FIRE AND REIGN

BRIDGETT EVANS

BEWITCHED PUBLISHING

Contact info:
www.instagram.com/bridgett_evans_author

Cover designed by: Elizabeth Cartwright of EC Editorial

ISBN: 979-8-218-10680-5

First Edition

Printed in the United States of America.
10 9 8 7 6 5 4 3 2 1

DEDICATION

To the Banana King, thanks for helping me rise
from the ashes

THIS BOOK CONTAINS

Abuse, choking, graphic sex, elements of dominance and submission, attempted sexual assault

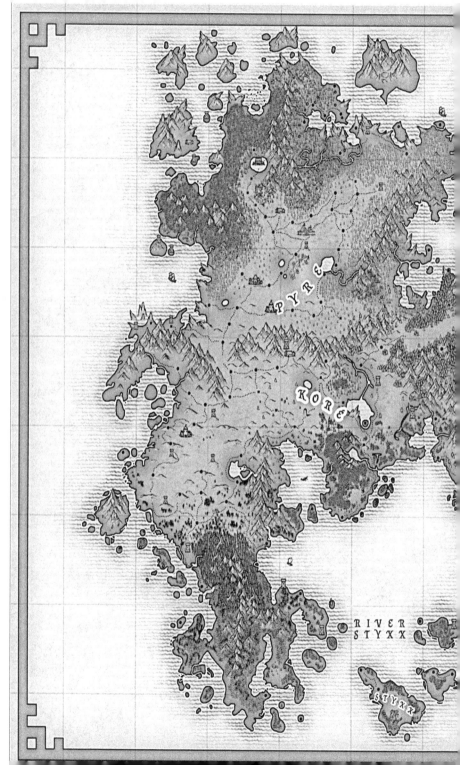

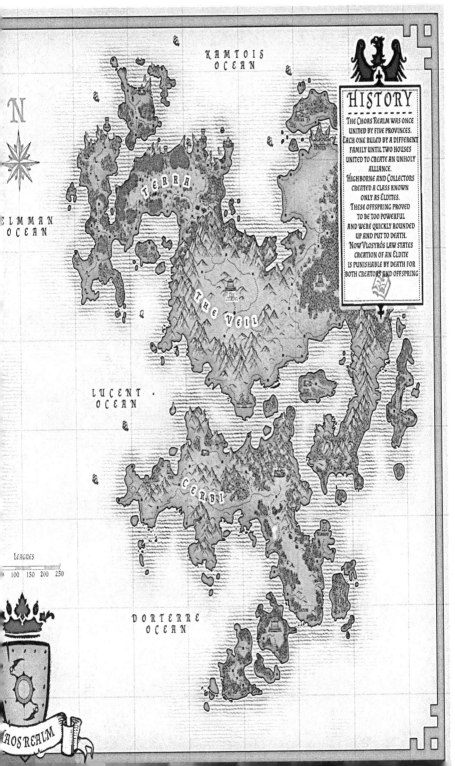

KAMTOIS
OCEAN

TERRA

LMMAN
OCEAN

THE VEIL

The Citadel

LUCENT
OCEAN

CERBI

Leagues

100 150 200 250

DORTERRE
OCEAN

N

HISTORY

The Chaos Realm was once
united by five provinces.
Each one ruled by a different
family until two houses
united to create an unholy
alliance.
Highborne and Collectors
created a class known
only as Eldites.
These offspring proved
to be too powerful
and were quickly rounded
up and put to death.
Now Vlosyrós law states
creation of an Eldite
is punishable by death for
both creators and offspring.

CHAOS REALM

PLAYLIST

Bury Me Face Down - grandson
Champions - Kurt Hugo Schneider, Andie Case
Born for this - CRMNL
Fire Meets Fate - Ruelle
Lover. Fighter - SVRCINA
Enemy - Imagine Dragons, JID
Play With Fire - Sam Tinnesz, Yacht Money
Animal - Riell, Jim Yosef
When We - Tank
Zipper - Jason Derulo
Mad - Imaginary After
Heaven - Julia Michaels
Middle of the Night - Elley Duhé
Darkside - Neoni, Besomorph Remix
Paranoia - Neon
Unstoppable - Sia, R3HAB Remix

GLOSSARY

Awakening 🔥 A rite of passage for all Highborne and Battleborne when they turn twenty-five years of age. Age of Awakening also symbolizes the ability to enter into a Contract with a male from an opposing House. It is also when latent abilities begin to awaken and female Highbornes fully mature.

Baphomet 🔥 Male witches for hire. Their bloodline is a mix of Highborne and Baphomet lineage. There are very few Baphomet in existence since the War of Realms wiped out a large population. Baphomets hold no allegiance to any Province but can be persuaded to help for a price. Baphomets can pass for Undesirables and choose to live their lives between all provinces. They are not the most trustworthy. *(Side note: They are the male counterparts of Beldames)*

Battleborne Lower class fire types that are normally outcast from their House due to the intermingling of bloodlines with Undesirables.

Beldame Female witches for hire, their bloodline is made of Beldames and Baphomet but has been diluted throughout the years by the bloodline of Undesirables after many of the Baphomet were wiped out during the War of Realms. It is unknown how many Beldames currently reside between Chaos and Terra. Beldames can pass for Undesirables and choose to live their lives between all Provinces. They are not the most trustworthy. *(Side note: They are the female counterparts of Baphomets)*

Cerbi Province that houses Collectors.

Chaos Magic Also spelled Chaos Magick, is a contemporary magical practice and religious movement. The use of energy signatures pulled from living organisms, specifically Undesirables can be considered a slippery slope and was outlawed by the Tribunal after the War of Realms.

Class 🔥 A specific group of people that are composed of subclasses *(Side note: Highborne are a class of Fire types)*

Collected 🔥 the Collecting of an aura to take into the Veil and eventually to their proper House.

Collectors 🔥 Decedents of Adon, God of Souls recruited upon moving into the Veil. Fated to usher new souls into The Veil and House, depending on the color of their aura.

Conduits 🔥 Gateways used mostly by Collectors, Baphomet and Highbornes to leave Chaos and to Terra, also known as Earth.1

Contracts 🔥 A written agreement of the terms and conditions one must follow after joining bloodlines. Meant to protect female Highbornes once they reach the age of Awakening. The equivalent of a Human Prenup. Only males are obligated to sign Contracts. *(Side note: It is rare for a Highborne to be Contracted to a Battleborne.)*

Creators 🔥 Another name for parents.

Eldite 🔥 Someone born of Highborne and Collector bloodlines; thought to be the most dangerous of the bloodlines. *(Side note: The last Eldite was thought to have been killed and was also the reason the Province War started)*

Gnosis 🔥 An altered state of consciousness that is also a form of Chaos Magic. Usually used by Beldames to perform the Shift.

Highborne 🔥 Pureblood fire type who have continued their bloodlines without mingling with Undesirables

Houses 🔥 Each Province has a class made for that region. And within that Province each class contains at minimum three to four Houses. To keep peace families join via Contracts.

Oblivion 🔥 Exile to the Styxx Province, the province farthest from Terra; this Province is reserved for those who have broken the Laws of Vlosyrós or the Treaty of Pyre

Pyre 🔥 Province that houses Highborne and Battleborne

Reborn 🔥 Collectors are the only class that are given the option to walk both sides of the Veil. Although Beldames and Baphomet can also walk both sides of the Veil they do so because they are of mixed bloodlines with an Undesirable (a.k.a. Human)

Resurrected 🔥 Only Eldites pass into the Veil and then are able to return back to Terra. This ability keeps the population unstable. Add to that the unknown abilities and it makes the Tribunal and classes beyond the

Veil nervous

The Shift 🔥 An antiquated spell performed for the right price and the price is usually too high, that is why only a handful of them have been performed. (The price is a lifetime of servitude)

Sight 🔥 The ability to see auras

Styxx 🔥 Province that houses those banished to Oblivion; surrounded by pitch-black waters

Terra 🔥 Realm that houses Humans (Undesirables), Beldames, and Baphomets

Treaty of Pyre?

The Tribunal 🔥 A group of five elders who monitor the illegal use of abilities and uphold the Laws of Vlosyrós.

Undesirables 🔥 Another word for Humans or Terranean

The Veil 🔥 the space between Terra and the remaining Provinces in the Chaos Realm that prepares those unaware of magic of its existence.

Vlosyrós Codex 🔥 The book that Collectors possess that show what souls they must Collect. Each Collector's Codex contains different names. Collectors can only see the name of the aura they are meant to Collect unless the Tribunal intervenes, which is rare.

Vlosyrós Laws 🔥 Four laws all Collectors must

follow; established after rogue Collectors disrupted the harmony of the Veil.

Law one: Ye shall uphold order and bear witness to an Undesirable's life from afar.

Law two: Ye shall not attempt to change the destiny of those who await The Veil.

Law three: Those found guilty of Collecting an Undesirable prematurely will be banished to Styxx.

Law four: Creation of an Eldite is punishable by death for both Creators and Offspring.

Vlosyrós Laws

Law one:
Ye shall uphold order
and bear witness to an Undesirable's life from afar.

Law two:
Ye shall not attempt to change
the destiny of those who await The Veil.

Law three:
Those found guilty of Collecting an Undesirable
prematurely will be banished to Styxx.

Law four:
Creation of an Eldite is punishable by death
for both Creators and Offspring.

PROLOGUE

London Reign never felt more at peace than the day she died. Until her twenty-fifth birthday, she had wandered day to day in a fog, blanketed by doubt and self-loathing. She accepted each moment with grace. After all, that was what a lady did.

Surrounded by a world where she felt Black women were never on equal ground, London hid inside a fortress built with her own hands. She placed each brick meticulously to keep everyone out.

This was her downfall in the end. Little did she know, each brick caged her in with something she couldn't hide from.

And so, on her twenty-fifth birthday, she closed her eyes, made her wish, blew out her birthday candles—then promptly died.

Yes, death had embraced her like an old friend, and for the first time, she felt nothing. It was everything she never knew was missing. In the darkness, she was someone important and no one at the same time.

But like all good things in London's life, there was an expiration date. This time was no different, as air rushed back into her lungs.

Although darkness greeted her once more, it was not welcome. There was no peace in this darkness, only the smell of musky air and clay.

Tired limbs collided against an unyielding surface, bouncing off in a thud. London repeated the same motion with her arms until realization seeped in, and a scream pierced her ears, followed by a blinding glow.

Then darkness enveloped her again, this time against her will.

Help me!

Words trapped in her head bounced around unaware only London could hear them. They were trapped among a haze that refused to lift. The ache pulsated beneath her breast and sent shockwaves of electricity as she cautiously moved her arm away from her body. This time she met no resistance. Involuntary tears streamed from eyes already burning, refused to open of their own accord.

London didn't know where she was, but it couldn't be good. Any place involving a coffin never was.

Help me!

The thump, thump, thump roared over the frigid air, sitting on her bruised lungs. They didn't allow her to scream out for help the way she wanted. Instead, London battled with heavy lids as they fluttered rapidly. She begged the darkness to disappear just this one time. This was not the peace she had dreamed of. This was hell.

Ashes to ashes.

London's head snapped to the left, only to be greeted by her old friend, darkness. Tears streamed down her face accompanied by a burning sensation as her eyes remained opened, fluttering closed a moment later. London wanted to close her eyes once more and never open them.

Dust to dust.

Slender fingers clenched and released as she took in the grime covering her hands. It didn't belong to her. Couldn't belong to her.

But it did.

The roar in her head disappeared with each shallow breath until her eyes focused on what was before her. London's surroundings resembled a war zone covered in debris as her eyes zeroed in on the rectangular slab in front of her. Her name and birthdate were carved neatly in what appeared to be stone with the quote, "Whether we remain the ash or become the Phoenix, is up to us."

"Impossible." London's voice sounded foreign to her. The word had more raspiness to it than she remembered. It was one of the only things she could recall.

"I picked out the quote myself. Looks like you decided to rise from the ashes after all."

Anxiety erupted as a silhouette stepped from the shadows. London's hands raised to defend herself as her eyes flickered marigold.

"Calm down, I'm here to help."

Moonlight illuminated the umber complexion of the mystery woman before her. But even though adrenaline coursed through her, London's body instinctively relaxed. The woman held a shovel covered in soil and grass against her leg as if to use it in case something amiss was to happen.

"Help."

The word grated from cracked lips with renewed conviction as London moved to her knees. The shift in her weight forced her body to collapse to the soil and grass beneath her.

"I know you are confused. I've been where you are . . . well not exactly where you are, but I know what you are feeling."

"You don't—"

"I do. The pain, the flashes of images—I'm here to help." The words were cut short by the mystery woman as she reiterated her original point. But London held onto doubt with an iron grip. For the first time she allowed herself to take in the woman's appearance.

Her skin glowed among the moonlight as tightly coiled locks of hair moved with each breeze. For a moment, London imagined the woman's eyes flickered a color rivaling the sun. That idea quickly faded as London stared up into her dark eyes.

"How?" London needed to know how someone could help her in a situation as precarious as the one she was in. The word was no more than a whisper as it disappeared among the night breeze. Lots of things were lost here. What was one more word?

"We don't have time for the 'how' right now. We need to get out of here before the Tribunal knows about your existence."

The mystery woman spoke calmly as she released the shovel from her hands and grabbed London around the waist, lifting her. London's body was no longer in the grave, she was liberated from it. London's attempt to prop her body up failed while the rest of her body tried it's best to move.

Nothing.

The mystery woman released London and stood to her original height. "I know you have questions, and I promise to explain when we get home."

"Home?"

London knew she must sound like an invalid, but the mystery woman made no sense. Who was the Tribunal and where was home?

Silence lingered between the two women before the mystery woman said, "Name's Ruby. I figured you wouldn't just take my word for it. That's why I brought these."

London's eyes moved down to see Ruby holding a pocket sized compact. Ruby opened the round case to reveal a mirror inside, "Look."

London took the mirror along with what appeared to be a photograph. Her eyes shifted from her reflection to the wrinkled image before glancing back toward the mirror. Lines moved over the faces of both women in the image, but there was no doubt who either individual was.

"Okay," London murmured, eyes glued to what she saw.

"Okay," Ruby repeated.

Pain radiated through London's body as she tried and failed to stand on her own two feet alone.

"Let me." London wanted to hold on to her distrust, but she needed answers, now more than ever. It didn't help that Ruby gave her a photo of the two of them standing under a banner that read, "Happy Birthday, London."

It was the only memory not drenched in doubt. London remembered that life hadn't always been easy. And for the first time since she took the first pained breath inside what was to be her final resting place, London remembered the saying that was the bane of her existence.

All good things must come to an end.

ONE

Five Years Later

The subtle displacement of energy always lifted the hairs on the nape of his neck. If he closed his eyes and focused Kieran could feel the tingling travel to the tips of his fingers. It reminded him of being electrocuted. A sharp zap moved up his arm before settling over his heart.

Inhabitants of Cerbi described it a lot like falling in love. Kieran felt both electricity and love shared the same outcome. Death. In the end he would pass on the feeling for a more realistic expectation.

Kieran's breathing caught in his throat before his cadence changed once more. The small hitch was enough to throw him off balance. There was no other way to explain how he knew it, but there was no mistaking what had taken place. Someone had performed the Shift.

The Shift, a form of Chaos Magic called Gnosis, was only performed by Beldames. If Kieran believed rumors, it was said that the female witches practiced the Earth magic from the time they were old enough to speak. The Shift was only one spell in a long line of life-altering castings taught from generation to generation.

The price to perform the Shift was steep and never ended well. Most recipients resided within Terra. The rest of Chaos knew anyone dumb enough to seek the help of a Beldame never got what they bargained for unless they knew how to ask.

Stories involving the Shift started with the promise of a happily ever after and ended with bloodshed. Anyone who was well versed in all things Chaos knew that.

Kieran Alexander was familiar with the history of Beldames. He had been a Collector for almost four years and studied them extensively. He could remember the antiquated ceremony happening only once. The day he was recruited.

Anyone aware of the consequences refrained from asking a Beldame to perform the Shift, because like all magic it came with a price. The cost a lifetime of service. Many died waiting for their obligation to be fulfilled. Each made the mistake of underestimating a Beldame.

Hubris didn't stop any Beldame from coming to collect what was rightfully hers. There was no use refusing. A deal with a Beldame was always enforced.

During Kieran's training to become a Collector he was overwhelmed with tales of warriors and citizens of the Chaos Realm. Undesirables were forbidden to venture past their province line.

Anyone caught outside of Terra earned a one-way trip to the Citadel. There they were judged by each member of the Tribunal. It was their obligation to decide whether to enforce the Treaty of Pyre and give the Undesirable asylum in Koré or let them rot in a cell in Styxx.

"Yo, Alexander peep this."

The words cut through the fog settling over Kieran. His watch switched to four o'clock on the dot. He had officially been awake for twenty-two hours. Cobalt eyes moved around taking in his surroundings. Everything seemed the same on the surface.

Music blared through speakers tucked away in every corner of the club. Strobe lights danced across the empty floor centered among an array of freshly bussed tables.

Kieran's eyes moved to the elevated DJ booth to find it empty. The word Renegades illuminated in bright red neon lights. He wasn't sure whose idea it was for him to become a silent partner in a nightclub.

"Tick tock." There was the reminder. Kieran had almost forgotten about his best friend, but there was no way Jaxon would ever allow that to happen. So much for being hands off.

Kieran stood in the middle of Renegades five minutes past four silently wishing harm against Jaxon. Their best waitress had quit on short notice and Kieran had done the only thing he could think of. He rolled up the sleeves on his expensive dress shirt and began taking orders.

With the club officially closed all Kieran wanted to do was grab his shit and get home. "Buchanan, I don't have time for—"

"Yeah, yeah. I know. Yada yada yada sleep. But seriously come to the back and check this out."

How had he heard him?

New Balance sneakers beat the stained concrete floors to submission with muted thuds. Kieran was lucky he left his gym bag in his office. There was no way he would have survived the night in his patent leather loafers.

It also didn't help that he never wore jeans or anything resembling a t-shirt. Kieran was a man obsessed with fashion not comfort and his wardrobe reflected that sentiment.

Cobalt eyes moved toward the empty DJ booth once more before he walked past it and opened the door leading into the hallway.

Deliberately messy locks rounded out the heart throb appearance that he strived for. He looked like any other employee at Renegades, ripped from the pages of some well-known modeling agency.

From his chiseled jaw line to his flawless tanned skin, Kieran was breathtaking to watch, no matter what he wore.

"What the hell is all this?"

Three large screens displayed different vantage points of the nightclub. A better set up than Jaxon had possessed the week before. Better than Jaxon could afford. He hadn't asked Kieran for help getting the new system. That in itself worried Kieran.

"You like?" Jaxon moved his eyebrows up and down in an obnoxious fashion before he opened his arms towards his new prized possession.

"It looks great, but where did you get all of this? We can't afford a system this sophisticated."

"Friend of a friend knew a guy who gave me a great discount."

"What friend? I know all your friends."

"Not this one." It sounded like lies to Kieran's ears. If there was one thing he learned in his two years back in Terra, it was that there wasn't anything that Jaxon Buchanan couldn't get.

"Five finger discount?" The joke lingered in the air before Kieran's laughter disappeared and his smile faded. "Shit, seriously?!"

"I didn't ask questions. He quoted me a price. I paid the man to set it up and then bid him farewell. No muss, no fuss."

"Sounds illegal."

"I have a receipt."

"Shady alleyway men give out receipts now?" Kieran's eyebrows also moved up before he released a sigh and finished with, "The cops won't be looking for this will they?"

"Of course not," Jaxon huffed. "I don't think."

"Buchanan—"

"I love it when you say my name like that." Kieran tried his best not to laugh. This was a serious situation. He didn't need any unnecessary heat from the cops. It was enough he still had to pay his own personal Beldame to continue Vudeux, a form of Gnosis that altered perception.

It was the only thing giving him the illusion of wealth that allowed Renegades to remain afloat. Vudeux didn't take as much as a Shift, but it did require sacrifice. A few drops of blood, several strands of hair and currency to pull energy from.

Now his brother from another mother was telling him he let a shady character sell them stolen merchandise.

On more than one occasion the two were confused for actual brothers. Both stood over six feet tall with chiseled features. The only difference was the eye color.

While Kieran sported Cobalt blue eyes, Jaxon's were a baby blue. It wasn't astounding, but it was enough.

"And done! Check it."

"We don't have time for another one of your gimmicks. We need to come up with legitimate ways to bring money in and I need to sleep."

"Spare me the lecture. Besides, our meeting isn't for hours. Plenty of time to catch a nap."

"You know that's not enough sleep, right?"

"Isn't it?"

Silence lingered between the two men before Kieran let out another sigh. He stepped closer to the monitor Jaxon looked at while frantically tapping away at his keyboard.

"Have you been tempted today?" Redemption is one drink away?"

"Yeah. Since we're next to the Garden, I figured why not take advantage of our prime real estate. Also, try to say the last part without the question mark."

"I don't think I can because I'm confused."

"What better way to exploit the Garden's clientele than to invite them in to cleanse their dirty souls and forget the sins they've committed next door."

"Uh-huh."

Kieran didn't want to throw more gas on the fire. He needed to find a gentle way to let Jaxon know this was a bad idea. There was a reason Renegades and the Garden didn't mix. And that reason was six foot four inches and held a grudge.

"Let's admit it . . . we both know sins are committed there every day."

Jaxon wasn't wrong about that part. The girls in the Garden had a special way of making everything a little morally gray. Nothing illegal happened on the surface, but they sure made it seem like a crime by the time the patrons exited the doors.

"It's a strip club. I don't think you can erase what goes on in there with just one drink." Kieran wasn't sure an entire keg could do the job. "Besides, don't they serve alcohol in the Garden."

"Not anymore. Which means no libations for the patrons inside. Didn't Antonio tell you?"

"I've—"

"Never mind," Jaxon cut Kieran off with a nod of his head towards the monitor. "Keep reading."

Kieran's eyes slowly shifted from word to word until he reached the last sentence on the screen.

"Antonio agreed to this?"

"Yep."

They were dead men if Antonio had given this promotion the okay. No matter how much it scratched each other's back, this was suicide. Antonio "Saint" Santos knew what it meant to be put between a rock and a hard place. By letting Jaxon run this event for the only strip club in New Haven, he was asking for trouble.

"All of this?"

The smile on Jaxon's face told Kieran everything he needed to know. The triumphant way he said, "All of it," told Kieran the rest.

"You're a dead man. You know that right?"

Featuring the Queen of Sin herself—Chastity Belle! Come pray at her altar!

"Yet, I've never felt more alive."

"Seems risky," Kieran continued.

Because it was risky and Kieran already knew the outcome. Renegades might have a great location but that didn't give them a pass. What Kieran was really worried about was Mason. And he knew for a fact that the man everyone knew as Doc wouldn't see the good in flaunting Chastity around like a piece of meat.

"No risk, no reward. Right? Besides, flyers will be going out today."

This son of a bitch was serious.

"You know Doc is going to murder you? You know that right?"

"Whatever man. I know what you're thinking and don't. Besides, I'm not afraid of Doc. I can handle him."

"I hope so." The words were cut off by a surprise yawn.

"None of that."

"As much as I want to stay and watch this train wreck, I'm out."

"Tell your moms I said hey," Jaxon smiled, drawing out the word hey, while wiggling his eyebrows up and down.

"Dick."

"Only the best. That's what your moms said," Jaxon quipped before music blasted again, giving the Garden a run for its money.

Yeah. Doc was going to kill him.

Kieran just hoped he was around to get ring-side seats.

TWO

"You need to focus."

London hated when her mother said those words. What did she think she was doing? She sure as shit wasn't sleeping on the job. It wasn't her fault she couldn't harness her ability yet.

It was five years since her Resurrection, and life went back to what she remembered before her death. She was walking through life in a fog and her mother didn't seem to notice. Or maybe, she didn't care.

"I am focusing."

With a blast of white light, London was knocked off balance and landed unceremoniously on her ass. She needed to tighten her core like she was told time and time again.

"You aren't."

To say Fenix was difficult to harness would be an understatement. All inhabitants of Pyre were taught to harness their fire ability at the age of thirteen. Fenix came natural to most, but London still struggled to learn the basics.

London tried her best to use what elemental magic she could without tapping into some form of Chaos Magic. Magic she wasn't supposed to be able to tap into at all because only witches used spell work.

Chaos Magic was never used by Highbornes. This type of magic was only reserved for Beldames and their male counterparts Baphomet. The warlocks weren't as powerful as Beldames, but one still didn't fuck with a witch, no matter the gender.

Chaos Magic wasn't something to be taken lightly. London hid that she needed very little guidance to perform magic. Ruby would surely make her run if she found out.

"Look at the candle, London. I want you to hover your hand inches above it. Do you feel the heat? Do you feel it threatening to burn you?"

"Yes."

London could feel her skin heating up as she focused on the flame below. She hated this part, it always hurt like hell. Her mother chastised her each time, telling her it wouldn't hurt if she focused. Well, that was a lie.

"Now do it."

London heard her mother's whispered words as she put all her energy into her ability without success. This time she mumbled under her breath, "Incendius."

The flame traveled from the candle to her palm, transferring with ease. London's use of Oris, a singular incantation derived from Chaos Magic, had worked.

"Praise Adon, you did it!"

"I did it!"

You cheated.

London ignored the voice. She didn't want to consider what she did cheating. It was a victory. There were no rule books for Eldites. Nothing about her birthright or legacy. The only thing London had to go on was what her mother told her, and everything Ruby Reign said ended in bloodshed.

"Do it again."

All the air left London's lungs as she looked at the proud smile on her mother's face. She got her small win and she wanted to run with it. That small win, however, took everything out of London. What she needed now was a drink.

"How about we take a break instead," left London's mouth before she could take the words back. Ruby didn't believe in breaks.

"There is no such thing as breaks when you're on the run. Do you not remember law four?"

The words spilled from London's mouth just as her mother spoke.

"Creation of an Eldite is punishable by death for both Creators and Offspring."

She heard the same words for the past five years. She had heard them so much, that she became disillusioned by them. Five years and no one knocked on her door. No one came to drag her away.

Five years and London was still standing unharmed. Not one singe on her skin she hadn't caused on her own.

"Mom, I just want one night to feel like a real grown up. I'm almost thirty—"

"I'm trying to ensure you make it a few more months to your thirtieth birthday London. Trust me."

"Of course, I trust you, Mom."

But even trust had limits. London knew she would break those limits tonight as she hugged her mother tight and whispered, "Duerme."

London wasn't proud of her actions. She wasn't proud to watch her mother yawn and slowly turn to walk toward her bedroom. She hadn't tried this particular incantation before, but she was happy to see that it worked.

Mom - 0

Oris - 2

London used the Chaos Magic once before without any results. This time with a little more focus she finally succeeded. Now the only thing left to do was make a break for it.

The drive downtown took less time than London anticipated. Now she sat in her car contemplating what got her to this moment. She used Chaos Magic on family. Not just any family—her mother.

The air sat on London, forcing small gasps from her. All logic was forgotten as her nightmare became a reality. She was as bad as the Tribunal believed. She used the very magic they warned about without thinking, just like lore stated.

That was when the fire from her dreams snaked its way in. It begged her to drop her guard. Begged her to allow it to consume her.

London knew not to cave into its bullying. She didn't need the fire to survive. She despised it for always being there at the most inconvenient moments.

London's eyes closed involuntarily as her wall fell long enough to let the fire in. Now she was about to burn.

Darkness sat with her just at the edge of her endless agony. London didn't know how she knew it was a woman. What London did know was the woman's name eluded her.

She waited for London to silently slip under the waves of pain, beckoning her to let go and come with her.

But then London remembered why she couldn't allow that to happen, and the fire extinguished just as fast as it appeared. Just like she had practiced.

Muffled music greeted her ears as soon as the car door opened. Images of scantily clad women and heavily tattooed men stood out against the backdrop of neon lights.

"This was a mistake." She should have never thought this would work. London cursed under her breath as she placed her hand on the door to step back into her car.

London.

Panic welled up in her chest, the air around her heavy once more as her head whipped toward the crowd to find no one approached her. The only sight before her was the neon sign that read Renegades and a crowded parking lot.

London.

She knew that voice, even over the roar of the music. She would recognize it anywhere. A voice that greeted her five years before.

London.

More words followed her name. Words that meant nothing to her, each syllable foreign, mixed with harsh consonants and soft vowels.

"Xordano, Brix."

London's eyes fluttered closed for a brief second to regulate her breathing as she chanted under her breath, praying it worked.

Instead, when she opened her eyes, she was surrounded by darkness.

"Xordano."

There was that word again.

"Fuck!"

"I am sorry, I forgot that the language does not come to everyone instantly. For some, it comes in waves, but it will come."

London lowered her head and began to chant with renewed intensity until she heard the darkness whisper, "Welcome, Daughter or Xordano, Brix."

"Welcome?"

"Yes. To the Veil. My name is Khaiv, but everyone calls me Eve."

Eve spoke to her the way a mother would a child. Her voice was calm as she said the words that meant nothing to London.

When there was only silence, Eve continued, "I am surprised to see you here alone. I thought that Stone would be escorting you, but I guess—"

"Stone?" London interrupted.

"Yes. Your Collector."

"Collector, like a serial killer? Or a coin collector?" London played dumb. She knew all too well what a Collector was, but she only had one shot to get this right.

"I suppose you would call him a Reaper or Grim Reaper. Although those words are based mostly on myths created by Undesirables."

"Right?"

"Come," the voice echoed before a cloaked hand reached out.

Just breathe, damn it!

"The word Collector has always held negative connotations in Terra. Think of the Veil as a safe haven for Undesirables. I'm a representative for the province of Cerbi. The other four members of the Tribunal will help decide if your time in Terra earns you a spot in Koré or if you are fortunate enough to enter the Sanctum."

"Is there a third option?"

"Do not be afraid. Koré is not the province you believe it to be. There are jobs and riches that await you there if that is your destiny."

"And if my destiny is the Sanctum?"

"Not many are fortunate enough to be sent to the Sanctum. All inhabitants of Chaos live their life as normal until they expire."

"And then they go to Sanctum?"

The Sanctum was a tale London's mother told her after her Resurrection. No one had any real knowledge of the afterlife except the Tribunal, but the rumor said Adon himself greeted every new arrival.

London knew that the Sanctum did not await her. Nor did Koré. If she didn't find a way out quickly, Eve would find out her secret.

"Only those chosen may walk with Adon, god of light and darkness. Perhaps you will be lucky enough to meet him. Terra was once considered an ally to the rest of the realm until they betrayed the remaining four provinces. Your trial with the Tribunal is penance for your ancestors actions. I need you to come with me."

"Occultaré," London chanted under her breath, but nothing happened. The chant to conceal her presence from magic wasn't working.

"Over seven centuries ago, the Tribunal decided auras would be Collected to make way for those who come after."

"Occultaré."

"Think of this as the next chapter for you. The Tribunal is fair. You will have a life designed with you in mind."

"As nice as this sounds, and it sounds great," London broke in, "I think I'd like to go now."

Her statement was met with silence, followed by a cough and then another. Something was burning.

"Daughter?"

London's eyes moved down to see the fire was back, renewing some of her hope and instilling a new sense of fear.

"Impossible. You must come with me now!"

It was the first time Eve's voice had raised, which was London's cue to get the fuck out of this nightmare. Smoke filled her nostrils, leaving a trail of soot behind. The taste of ash mingled with the metallic taste of blood on her tongue. It was the only thing she needed to ensure the chant was effective.

All magic had a price. This was small in comparison to what she already sacrificed.

"Daughter, you must come with me now under breach of law four under the Vlosyrós Law."

Anger replaced fear at the sound of the word *daughter*. White ribbons became visible for the first time as London's eyes roamed the darkness and saw nothing. She was the daughter of Ruby Reign!

"Occultaré!"

"NO!"

London heard the frustration in Eve's voice as the radiant white light flashed before her.

Music came rushing back along with the distant sound of yelling.

"You okay?" a masculine voice asked. Cobalt eyes stared into hers with intensity. For a moment London forgot to speak and only nodded.

"God, you scared me," London heard before her eyes drifted closed and her body became limp.

"Did you get him?"

"Negative. He was gone once I hit the street. He must have had a driver waiting for him."

"Fuck!"

The voices sounded close. Voices that were different from the darkness.

Eve.

"Did you see her hands?"

"No. I was busy trying to make sure she didn't crack her skull on the pavement."

Were they talking about her?

"Ouch," London groaned as she moved her arm to push against the surface beneath her.

"She's awake!"

London's eyes stared as the navy button up hugged what appeared to be a very fit man. Instantly realizing she was too close, she attempted to move away but collided with a literal wall. London's head throbbed as she angled her neck to look at his face.

He's tall.

And then her eyes focused on him. The very definition of Adonis, from his blue eyes to his blond hair.

"Sorry."

"No, I'm sorry for yelling," his voice was laced with concern, "You caught us off guard."

"Us?"

London's eyes traveled down his body and back up before she saw someone standing behind him.

"Hi," another handsome man answered with a quick wave.

"What's your name?"

"What?" London asked, diverting her attention back to the man before her.

"Do you know your name? The year?" Adonis asked.

"Yeah. I'm fine. Just a headache."

"You went down pretty hard. Plus you did get mugged. I'm Kieran," the Adonis offered before pointing toward the man behind him, "That's Jaxon."

"Pleasure," Jaxon smiled with the nod of his head.

Is that what Eve made them think?

"Not to sound creepy," Kieran started effectively blocking her escape, "but I was watching you earlier—"

"It's a little creepy, Kieran," London interrupted. She needed to get the fuck out of here.

"Right. I thought about inviting you in, but then you ran toward the alley."

"Thought I heard something," London whispered with the hope he believed her.

"So you ran *toward* the alley?"

"To be fair, I didn't think. I just reacted," London answered attempting to stand again.

"Whoa, just sit here for a minute," Kieran rushed, guiding her back toward the floor.

"I'm fine."

"I'm sure you are but humor me. Okay?"

"I don't know you."

"Remember, I'm Kieran," his lips pulled back, revealing the most seductive smile she had seen.

"Kieran—"

"And you are…?"

"Leaving soon unless you can offer me a job. That's why I was outside the club."

"What kind of job?" Jaxon's voice broke through the fog blanketing her. "Cuz' I have a spot for a waitress. The job starts tonight if you want it."

"Seriously?"

"Hell yeah! I mean, yes," Jaxon exclaimed before dialing it back a little.

London's eyes moved between the two men before Jaxon spoke again, "What do you say?"

"Hell yeah." Freedom was one step closer, but there was the problem of Eve. There was no denying she had seen her use Fenix. London knew she would have to do damage control. With any luck Eve wouldn't know where to start looking to find her.

"Did I walk in on something?" a new voice interrupted. All eyes moved toward the intrusion.

"I think this calls for a drink!" Jaxon exclaimed instead of answering.

The new mystery man didn't move, his eyes fixated on London. Did only hot guys work in this club? London took in his appearance and tried her best not to stare.

"Who's the new girl?" Mystery man three asked. He didn't look like the two men London saw when she opened her eyes. His hair was different and his eyes were green—not blue.

"This is our new waitress. What's your name sweetheart?"

"London."

"Nice. I'm Simon," green eyes volunteered.

"What's your poison, Lonny?"

"Bourbon," London ignored Jaxon's pet name. Her eyes shifted back to Kieran to see him staring at her making her heart flutter.

"Just like Stone," Simon chuckled as he moved toward the bar to watch Jaxon attempt and fail to juggle two large bottles before pouring four shots.

"Stone?"

"Yeah, that's what Kieran's boss calls him sometimes, among other names," Simon laughed.

"You work here too?" London directed her question toward Kieran, but before he could answer Jaxon beat him to it.

"He's part owner of Renegades."

"Oh."

"Silent partner."

"Yeah, yeah, yeah."

"He can be a real hard ass sometimes, so it fits," Simon offered."

I thought that Stone would be escorting you.

"Interesting," London whispered as she grabbed the shot being offered to her by Simon.

"Salud," Kieran whispered before downing his shot. "Salud."

London reveled in the burn of the liquid as it traveled down her throat. If this was the same person Eve spoke of, then she was in deep shit.

THREE

Kieran couldn't put his finger on the feeling clawing just beneath the surface. He spent fourteen days combing through information and found nada, nothing, zilch. Two weeks of looking at information only to find out there was nothing out of the ordinary. Deep down he knew there was something off about his new employee London. He just needed some hard evidence to confirm his suspicions.

On the surface everything was spotless. She'd never even had a parking ticket, but that was the problem. London's background was too clean. She was a twenty-nine-year-old woman, about to turn thirty, with limited college education and no work history. Her only living relative seemed to be her mother, and even information on that front turned up dry.

It took him weeks to find out that on the surface London Reign was practically a saint. And Kieran didn't believe in saints.

"You're staring again."

"I'm observing," Kieran responded to Jaxon without taking his eyes off of London. He was in fact staring, but not for the reasons that Jaxon believed. "Just trying to be more hands on."

"I thought you were a silent partner."

Kieran's eyes shot to Jaxon to find a smug look of satisfaction where there should be agreement. The slight red tinge to his friends face pissed Kieran off as Jaxon doubled over trying to keep quiet. "You fucking serious?"

"Never," was the only response that Kieran received. "Besides you keep eye fucking London and she might form an official complaint to me."

"Eye fucking? I'm just—"

"Observing."

"Right." Kieran could tell his answer did nothing to stave off the childish imagination he knew his partner and best friend, must be coming up with. Kieran was obsessing over London's presence in Renegades.

"I'm gonna go and see if she needs any help."

"Kieran, I don't think that's a good idea."

"To help an employee?" Kieran's body had already began moving of its own volition as he made his way towards London.

"To—and he's gone."

Kieran pretended to not hear Jaxon's words, but he needed to figure out what this itch beneath the surface was that took hold of him. It wasn't lust, couldn't be. Even if he did find London to be his type, Kieran knew deep down that she was hiding something, and that took precedent.

"London, how's training going?"

"Shit!"

The look on London's face made Kieran smirk himself as he watched her hand move above her heaving breasts. She was genuinely scared and there was a primal part of Kieran that loved it. He could see potential where there shouldn't be any and for a moment it excited him. That was until he heard London chuckle and remembered why he was standing before her.

"Um, good, Mr. Alexander."

"Please, call me Kieran."

"Right. Kieran. It's going okay. Savannah has been a great help with teaching me the numbering system for the tables and how to avoid taking a shot."

Kieran's brows lifted at the sound of taking shots on the clock. He knew that it was a joke, but he didn't joke when it came to his money. And jokes about drinking on the job were never tolerated when he was at work. Jaxon might let that shit go, but he wasn't Jaxon.

"Avoid taking a shot?"

"I mean—"

"I know what you mean."

Kieran couldn't help the brash tone that came out, he wanted to tease her just a little before he put on the real pressure. But that went out the window in an instant. Instead, he took in London's appearance. She was dressed professionally enough for training in a nightclub.

Her hair was pulled into a messy bun at the base of her neck. What he had come to realize as her standard white tee clung to her body revealing just enough to separate her from the girls at The Garden. Kieran would gladly pay to pray at her altar instead under the right circumstances.

"I apologize for how that sounded, sir."

Sir. He liked the sound of that. In another life Kieran reveled enjoyed being called Sir. He had let the word pour over him like warm whiskey. But that life was over in an instant and his mission in life changed in a blink of an eye. His job now was to sit and wait. The reason didn't matter and asking questions wasn't an option.

"London, I wanted to ask you a few questions about your background check."

"Yes?"

For a brief moment Kieran could see panic laced with genuine interest cross London's face. She placed her hands behind her back like a soldier waiting on orders. Had she been in the military or was it just a defense mechanism? That move added more questions to Kieran's list than the answers he already had.

"It says you have no work history. I was just curious, how that is possible?"

"I've never needed to work," was the only response, followed by silence.

"Never?"

"Never?" London repeated.

"No, Sir."

There was the word again. Kieran cleared his throat, his hands shoved into his pockets. Any more use of that word and he might not be able to control what happened next. Consequences be damned.

That's creepy.

"We typically need a couple of references for new hires. Maybe you've had a summer job or internship we could use. Anyone to vouch for your work ethic?"

Something!

"No. My family has done pretty well for themselves and I've never needed to work. But I really needed this job."

"Is that so?"

"Yes, Sir."

"London, you don't have to call me Sir. Kieran is fine."

"Right."

He knew he was never going to get far with her if she considered this to be an interrogation. Which it was.

But to gain her trust he would need to change his tactics. He needed for London to view him as more than her employer. Kieran took two steps backwards to give London the illusion of space. Maybe then she would relax and open up.

No luck, this only caused her body to tense more.

"If your family is well off, why do you need a job waitressing of all things? Doesn't your family think this is a step down?"

"It's your place. Do you think it's a step down?"

Check. She was good.

"Of course not. But I'd imagine someone with the resources you allude to wouldn't want their daughter working in such an establishment."

For a moment Kieran thought he had her right where he wanted her. Until she said, "My mother doesn't know."

Damn it. She has an answer for everything.

"So don't contact her as a reference? Her number popped up while doing the background check."

"NO!"

Checkmate.

"I apologize. I didn't mean to strike a nerve."

"You didn't, but my mother really doesn't know. I'd like to keep it that way."

"Of course. I should probably let you get back to work. I just had one more question—"

"Oblivii."

Kieran's expression quickly changed as he listened to the incantation. A frown crossed his face which allowed London to relax. Had she just tried to spell him? Of course she was a Beldame, that explained everything.

He would play along for the time being. If he said anything now she would know that most forms of Chaos Magic, including Oris didn't work on Collectors. For the time being Kieran would let Ms. Reign believe she had made him forget their current conversation.

"I'm sorry. What did you say?"

"Thank you, Mr. Alexander. I'll try to remember to turn in my information to allow Renegades to pay me directly."

No. Thank you.

"Kieran."

"Right. Kieran."

With a nod, Kieran turned his back to London. His steps clashed against the stained concrete as he walked back toward Jaxon who pretended to be looking at new inventory.

"You can stop 'working' and follow me."

"I am working."

Kieran's body instantly moved pass the bar and opened the door leading to the hallway past the DJ booth. He couldn't tell Jaxon anything but they had more important things to talk about anyway. London Reign would just have to wait until he could figure out what House she belonged to.

"What did she say?"

"Who?"

"Who? London, that's who!" Jaxon's tone bordered on laughter and indignation.

"Nothing of any importance."

"Kieran—"

"What we really need to be talking about is Georgia Rae Devereux and After Dark Bar and Grill."

Jaxon knew what Kieran said was true. They had put off the acquisition of the establishment for far too long. Renegades had a reputation for being raunchy and After Dark's clientele could change that for them. What they couldn't do on their own, Georgia Rae Devereux could help with.

"She's never committed."

"Then we need to make her."

"Make her? Have you met her?"

"No. But everyone has something they want. We just have to find something to tempt a Devereux." Kieran was adamant that everyone had some kind of tell or ask. He hadn't met a single person who didn't want something from him out of life. Georgia Rae was no exception. All he needed to do was find out that one thing.

"We can call her assistant, Amelia."

"That's good. We can have Savannah do that."

Kieran could see the confusion on Jaxon's face as he asked, "Why Savannah?"

"Because if Georgia Rae has an assistant then we have to show her that we do as well. It's all a power play with families like hers, believe me. If she thinks we are too busy to even make a phone call, her interest will be piqued."

"Okay. I'll let you do what you do best. You didn't make your fortune by not knowing what you're doing."

A fortune spelled to him. But what good would having all that money be for him if he didn't help out the one person he had come to call a brother?

"Let's get Savannah in here, I guess."

"Perfect." He could see it now. After Dark was as good as Kieran's.

FOUR

Two weeks passed since she come face to face with the darkness named Eve and lived to tell the tale. Two weeks since she had inadvertently given herself away and waited with bated breath for Collectors to come for her.

And in all that time, she hadn't thought it was important enough to clue in her mother, Ruby. London knew what she would say, knew what she would do, and she wasn't willing to risk that.

After the interrogation with Kieran, London was sure he knew something. Her use of Oris had gotten better since she knew what emotion to tap into. Fear was always unpredictable. Self-preservation was much more powerful.

For the rest of the night London had kept a close eye on Kieran, a.k.a. Stone. He hadn't given any indication he had remembered their conversation. Nor did it appear he knew what she really was. An Eldite.

The spell had worked, and all was right with the world. She had a job she actually liked and her freedom. What could go wrong?

"London?"

She had spoken too soon. London's hand moved to her chest, labored breathing escaping parted lips. London ensured she kept her distance from Kieran just to be safe and to her surprise he had done the same. Her mother was a different story.

London's eyes moved towards the kitchen to find her mother standing near the island in the middle of the room. She took in the woman who had given her life and provided for her against all odds. Long ebony locks fell against her bosom. Different from the first time she saw her after her Resurrection.

Various scenarios raced through London's head. Her mother never saw her come in this late. Would she ask where London had been? Now was not time to analyze the situation. It was a time for sleep, but all that was out the window now.

"You're up."

What had she done to deserve this living hell? The rhetorical question lingered in the air as she looked at her mother. There she was staring London in the face, smiling at her with an unprecedented amount of love. She was a horrible daughter and she knew it. London had used Chaos Magic on her mother and now she was hiding the one thing that would send Ruby through the roof.

"Well, it is after seven—"

"Right," was the only reply London gave until the uncomfortable silence kicked in. She needed a different word to use when she was caught in a web of lies.

Ruby's presence always filled any room she inhabited. Even her clothing screamed confidence because Ruby Reign went big with everything she did.

"I made breakfast, but it's probably cold. French toast."

"I'm not hungry. I was gonna head up to bed, but maybe later?"

"You've been sleeping in a lot. Staying out late." London now knew that her mother had noticed her absence.

"I apologize if I've worried you."

"I'm your mother. Of course, I worry."

"I'll try to stay home at night more. Promise." London's lie came out like butter. She was getting better at being deceptive. And while it should cause her stomach to turn, London felt nothing.

When Ruby didn't protest, London took that as her cue to escape the increasingly awkward interaction.

"Spoke to Theresa Bellicose."

There it was. The words London hoped to never hear. After months of nothing, she was sure she had gotten away with it. She was wrong.

"Oh?"

"Yeah. Did you know we go to the same book club? I've been MIA for a while but decided to stop making excuses and go."

"I didn't know you went to book club."

"Haven't been in about a month, with work and volunteering…anyway, she asked about you."

"That's nice." London knew what was coming and braced for impact to lessen the fallout.

"Yeah. She wanted to know why you wanted a spell since we are Highbornes."

"What did you tell her?"

"That you wanted to know more about Beldames. I told her you were curious about the components of an incantation."

"I see."

"She was happy to help with a lesson about her class."

"Good."

"Crazy thing is that I don't remember you telling me about a spell. And I couldn't let her know my daughter was using Oris behind my back!"

The anger rolled off Ruby in waves, the heat radiating from her skin was enough to form sweat droplets on London's forehead. Ruby was pissed.

"I know you are upset—"

"No! Upset is when you stay out all night and don't call. Upset is the time you caught the house on fire. This! This is me being infuriated! What did you do?!"

Each word was said louder until the lights flickered and then went out.

"Lux," London whispered the word and all lights flickered back to life. She was already caught, there was no need to continue lying. She had spent months befriending the Bellicose's daughter after Ruby mentioned the family was from a well-respected house of Beldames.

After some research, London discovered the Bellicose family belonged to the most powerful house of Beldames in all of Chaos. Other Beldames sent their children to a Bellicose to be trained. And if they were that good, London wanted to learn any magic she could from the best.

All it took was piqued interest in all things spiritual, and she was in like Flynn. Ruby explained to London months after her Resurrection everything would be different. One of those things was the manipulation of energy, and magic was all energy when she thought about it.

The only problem was Highbornes weren't supposed to be able to do magic. An ability like Fenix was different. All Highborne and Battleborne developed their abilities at the age of thirteen. Until their twenty-fifth birthday they studied the history of Pyre and trained to be of service if the time ever came.

London's family house would never be called to war if time came. A Reign was the reason others in Pyre fought in their place. Ninnie Reign had ensured her family rose to great power long after the Treaty of Pyre was signed.

Royal blood ran through London's veins and she would never reap the benefits. Not because she wasn't a Highborne, but because she wasn't only a Highborne. Her bloodline had been tainted by a Collector.

London belonged nowhere. She was an Eldite. By default she was a dead woman walking.

An Eldite didn't need to be a Beldame to do incantations. They only needed the correct ingredients, an offering, and a shit ton of focus. London was still working on the last part.

"I may have been practicing Chaos Magic for a few months."

"That's impossible."

"It was simple enough to learn some of the incantations—"

"Highbornes can't do magic!"

"I'm not a Highborne!"

Silence filled the room as London watched her mother's eyes glow marigold. Her focus shifted to the French toast before moving back to look at London.

"I know you aren't a Highborne. But I am. As my daughter you should never be able to successfully perform any form of Chaos Magic, whether it be Oris or Gnosis."

"Theresa doesn't know that I have been successful."

"London, I told you that you would need to harness your ability. You need to be able to protect yourself and five years is too long for you to still be at the level you are at."

"I'm trying, Mom."

"I know, baby. But something is holding you back. No more magic. Highbornes can't do spells and to those that matter you are a Highborne and that is all."

"But—"

"End of story."

"Not end of story."

"I've dreaded this moment since you turned sixteen. Since you were born really," the sound of Ruby's voice became less tense as her bottom hit the bar stool with a light thud.

"When I was sixteen. That was when I—"

"That was when WE figured out that some things don't skip generations."

"Right."

The tears were right there but London wouldn't dare let them fall. She had two years to come to grips with her past, now was not a time to let those emotions out. Not when she was working on her self-control. This subject always tested her control.

"I wanted to shield you from our world. After the fire—after everything, I should have explained everything to you. I should have sat you down and come up with a game plan. Part of me thought if I ignored it, then it wasn't real. I think I was still in denial."

"It's understandable."

"Don't do that." Burnt orange irises stood out against ivory orbs that peered into her soul and then were gone with the blink of an eye.

"Sorry," was the only response London could muster.

"It was supposed to manifest on your thirteenth birthday. But your birthday was uneventful and part of me was relieved. You hadn't exhibited any signs that would prepare me for—." Ruby's voice trailed off as she looked at London's eyes move towards her clasped hands.

"Go on, please."

"Your father was supposed to be from Terra. He never gave any inclinations of being anything else. And there were rumors that anyone who created life with an Undesirable doomed their offspring to a fate of mediocrity. I was okay with that."

"Adon, I hate that term." It made everyone in Terra sound like trash. Even if she wasn't an Undesirable, it was still awful.

"Adon was exactly who I prayed to the moment I found out I was pregnant with you.

When my mother didn't show up unexpectedly, I was elated. It meant that I had truly escaped her and my royal obligation. You could live a normal life. Then you turned sixteen."

"And I burned your world down, literally." London's sadness deepened as her mother recounted one of their most painful memories.

"I got scared when I saw it. I froze," Ruby continued, "but not your father. He grabbed you and held on tight. He wasn't afraid of the fire. He just wanted to make sure his little girl didn't burn. And you didn't."

"But he did." The strained words hit harder every time London said them.

"You passed out from the exertion. The first time is like that, and I was thankful. It allowed me to call Rissa Sampson."

"My history teacher?"

She's a Beldame. She had questions about the incident. Questions I managed to answer through my panic."

"Mrs. Sampson is a Beldame?"

"Not everyone in Terra is an Undesirable. You should know this."

"It doesn't make it less shocking, Mother."

"She was able to give you something to keep you asleep until we could figure out what to tell you," Ruby continued.

"That's a lot to deal with Mom."

"She's the reason some of your memories are jumbled to this day. Some memories are too dangerous to recall."

"You told me that after my Resurrection my memories would take time to return."

"That part is true. Lore states that after Resurrection, that your memories would be lost to you at first and would come back in waves or broken pictures. Was that not true?"

"It was, but some make no sense."

"That is my fault. It took some misdirection to spin my story, but Rissa fell for it. As a mother, she sympathized with me. A mother will do anything to protect her child from that kind of pain."

Silence lingered between the two of them. The pregnant pause expanded by the moment until finally, it popped.

"Your grandmother once told me she prayed I never knew the burden of lying to my child. Of course, I didn't listen. I was twenty and my Awakening wasn't for years. I was too young to think about children."

Ruby's laughter didn't reach her eyes as they shifted down to her clenched fists. "But Jacqueline Reign wasn't going to let that be my truth. Of the four families of Highborne, two remained pure, and I was the next heir contracted to carry on the Reign legacy."

"Contracted? Married off like cattle you mean."

"The same as any other business venture. Contracts are like a prenup in a way. It helps protect against any damage to the reputation of the female involved. I was the only unattached female left in the family fated to marry Phillip Andilet."

"Twenty-five is kind of young to marry, isn't it?"

"Tradition is tradition in Pyre," was the only answer London received.

"Some traditions are meant to be broken," London whispered reeling from her mother's cavalier tone.

"As a child, every Highborne is educated in the history of their bloodline. The people of Pyre told stories of war and honor that made them sound like a fairytale.

And then I grew up and realized the weight my last name bore. Married off to ensure peace would continue for everyone in Chaos. Everyone but myself."

"That sounds like a miserable existence."

"Any other female would kill to be put in my predicament, but I wasn't on board with shackling myself to a male unless I deemed him worthy. Not because of the blood flowing through his veins."

"What happened next?"

"The night of my Awakening, I used a Conduit to sneak into Terra and I met your father."

"Lucas St. Claire." London smiled thinking of father.

"Yeah, Lucas St. Claire. Sounds like a regal name, right?" Ruby laughed.

"But dad wasn't an Undesirable," London frowned at the word, its syllables tasted like the soot that filled her nostrils and mouth sometimes, "Which explains how I am who I am."

"Correct," she heard her mother say, "It does."

"I'm an Eldite. I know that. Then why do I still feel like an Undesirable?"

The word hurt to say every time. If Highbornes were Pyre royalty and her father's bloodline was unknown to her, then London figured she was probably the garbage they threw away.

"Highbornes don't need to be Resurrected after their Awakening. Until you, I prayed it wasn't true, but then you died unexpectedly, and I knew. So, I did what any grieving mother should do. I worked fast to have your funeral. Then I waited."

London's breath came out in spurts as she looked into similar eyes. "You buried me."

"Yes."

"Why? Why not wait the five days it would take for me to resurrect and do the Shift."

"Because it was the difference between life and death. Which makes what I have to say next hard."

London braced herself for the next words to leave her mother's mouth. The lights flickered once more but remained on as Ruby took a step towards her daughter.

"Your father is alive, London."

"What?"

The air left London like she had been sucker punched. Her chestnut brown eyes moved over her mother's face looking for deception. She found none.

"When I met him, I didn't know he was a Collector, and he didn't know I was a Highborne. Rissa owed me a favor, and she changed my aura from orange to green way before I met your father to escape Pyre. Green, the aura of Terra."

And just like that, the room moved in on London, and all sound disappeared. Her father was alive? She hadn't killed him.

"Where is he?"

"I don't know. When I got the flames under control, my first thought was the worst. But there he stood, clenching you in his arms. Not a mark on his body. It was then that we both knew we were screwed."

"Law four. Creation of an Eldite is punishable by death for both Creators and Offspring," London whispered. Those words never meant anything before. Every class had a weakness and death was universal or so London thought.

"Yes."

"Murdered. All of us."

"Yes," Ruby repeated.

"Where is he?" London asked for a second time as if the first time hadn't been enough. She needed to find the man who made up half her genetic makeup. She craved information that her mother could never provide. Would not provide.

Her father was alive.

"I don't know. He left once the realization sunk in. His only advice was to run. Run and never look back."

"But you didn't."

"No, I didn't," Ruby agreed. "I did something far worse."

London felt nothing for the first time since she Resurrected. She was the daughter of a Highborne and Collector, she knew that. This new information added a new level of holy shit to her world. Her father was alive.

"London."

"The Shift?"

"Yes." Ruby's answer was short and to the point.

"I'm not running."

"I would have agreed before, but you're using Chaos Magic."

"I can fix this."

"Law four—"

"I know what law four says Mother."

"London—"

"Oblivii."

The spell wouldn't make Ruby forget everything, only the last hour. She'd still remember the conversation with Theresa, but at least London knew what lie to tell now.

"London?" Ruby's eyes blinked as she stood and walked towards her. "Did you just get here? I made breakfast, it's probably cold by now."

"Yeah, sorry Mom, lost track of time."

"Well come sit with me. We have something to talk about."

"I'm actually gonna head upstairs."

"Nonsense. Sit down."

London watched her mother put her plate in the microwave to warm it up. A plan already formulating in her head. If her father was a Collector, she would bet anything another Collector might know how to find him.

It looked like getting close to Kieran was in the cards after all. London just needed to be careful. One slip up, and they were all as good as dead.

FIVE

"Whores get paid to fuck, and I ain't fucking you."

The words erupted louder than Kieran expected as laughter filled the space. Chastity was her name but she was anything but chaste. Her body moved away from the customer with grace, snatching the currency from his hand accompanied by the push of the head.

Kieran stopped pretending to be shocked by the words that escaped Chastity's mouth. He was honestly surprised those were the only words that tumbled from her mouth as he watched Chastity glide to the opposite side of the stage.

Chastity Belle was nothing if not a true entertainer. She even made a show out of tucking the twenty-dollar bill she liberated between the thin line of her G-string and hip.

Her ass jiggled just enough as she rolled her body to the music. Chastity was a veteran at the Garden. She worked in the club for as long as Kieran had been top side in New Haven. Everyone knew Chastity wasn't afraid to show off the curves that god had given her.

A different beat slowly faded in, letting the patrons know that the infamous Chastity Belle's set was officially done.

"If you haven't gotten enough of the Queen of Sin, she'll be heading next door to Renegades shortly. Those who wish to pray at her altar need to be in line by midnight with the flyer you received at the door. But if you want to see what else the Garden has in store for you tonight then stay your ass right here. With all the sin you just witnessed, why don't I give you a little piece of Heaven!"

The new girl, Heaven, now held everyone's attention. She quickly bent at the waist and gracefully popped back up, only to drop it low just as the song suggested. The form was a little stiff, but management wasn't looking for the next Ginger Rogers or Beyoncé. The only people she needed to impress were the sea of horny men practically drooling at her feet.

Amateurs.

"Yo, Tonio! You closing?"

"Always. Why? Do you need something?"

When didn't Kieran need something?

Antonio was the exact opposite of Kieran. Where Kieran had blue eyes and blonde hair, Antonio rocked his hair dark brown with even darker eyes. He had dubbed himself the Latin Lover years before Kieran had met him. It killed him to admit the title was well deserved. Antonio had a way with the ladies Kieran couldn't help but appreciate.

"Just watching your girl."

"Not my girl!" Antonio shouted over the music, "Doc's!"

"I thought they were through."

"Tell that to Doc," Antonio laughed; his eyes focused on the dance floor.

Kieran's eyes moved over the crowd as music poured in around him. His eyes moved over each person in attendance. He clocked three Collectors among the crowd, their auras black as night among a sea of green.

All Collectors had the ability of Sight and could see the auras of every class. Terra was green and Cerbi, where he came from, was black.

There was no telling who the poor bastards being Collected were. Their fates were sealed for at least a week when their names appeared in someone's Codex.

It was every Collectors sworn duty as a son or daughter of Adon to ensure their Undesirable was escorted safely to the Veil. Kieran could still feel the Papyrus crinkle softly beneath his fingers. Each sheet graffitied with the latest list of names. Next to each entry was a category to help every Collector prepare for what was to come. The gender, location, and a brief description of the inciting incident was scrawled haphazardly across the beige paper.

"May Adon be with you." It was all in his hands now.

"What was that?!"

"Nothing!"

It looked like the Veil would be getting a few new occupants, and Kieran wouldn't be in Cerbi to hear about it. He was stuck in Terra, being useless.

"Well, I'm out." Kieran was on a time crunch and already spent too much time at the Garden. Part of him thought he might catch a glimpse of Doc. Kieran was surprised when it appeared he hadn't shown up for the promotion after all.

"Heading back to Renegades?"

"You know it."

"Don't you ever take a day off?"

Antonio's question was valid, but tonight was different. Tonight he had a date. If he couldn't do his actual work, he might as well distract himself, and what better way to do that than getting lost in someone else? Plus, he needed to get laid.

"For pleasure, not business," he answered causing Antonio to redirect his attention.

"Okay! I see you!" Antonio approved with a high-five, "Don't bring no babies up in here!"

"Fucking asshole. Don't get in too much trouble." *Leave it to Antonio*, Kieran thought, turning his back to move through a sea of sweaty bodies.

"They don't call me Saint for no reason." His laughter blending with the music.

"Asshole." Kieran whispered to himself, the music blaring louder as he heard the words, "Make some mother fucking noise!"

Even with the promise of a good night, Kieran couldn't ignore the nagging feeling of doom pulling at him. If there was one thing he learned years ago, it was to never ignore that feeling. It was always a precursor for destruction.

Renegades was packed.

Of course, it was. Chastity set up a table for autographs by Jaxon's DJ booth. And the crowd flocked to her.

"Alexander!"

Kieran's eyes searched for Jaxon to see he was behind the bar. For someone who was a part owner, he never delegated anything. Even when Kieran had offered to help, it was turned down. Jaxon didn't want Kieran around for help, he wanted him there because it was his will.

Years of Gnosis made sure of that. Kieran quickly become acquainted with the form of Chaos Magic while training in the Citadel. The domed building resembled a work of art. Depictions of the Province War told a story of how Terra came to be torn from the other provinces of Chaos. It was how the practice earned its name.

Orientation for a Collector comprised of meeting Eve, their boss. Becoming a Collector felt more like a dream than reality. One moment he was moving about his day and the next he was standing in a chasm of darkness that spanned further than the eye could see.

Was this death?

The answer was no. It was a reprieve. Death was knocking on his door, but someone saw potential in him. And so Kieran was presented with two scenarios. He could be returned to his everyday life where his life would end in tragedy or he could give his life over to Adon and help usher auras into the Veil.

Kieran chose the second option unaware that death would never knock on his door again. And so a Shift was performed to erase his existence from Terra completely. To the world Kieran Alexander never existed.

Eve explained how each new soul would be given their own orientation to explain their new life. Collecting wasn't reserved to only Undesirables. All classes in Chaos were at the mercy of Collectors.

Each person was escorted to the Citadel where a council of their peers decided their fate.

That was four years ago, and this was Kieran's first official assignment. On the surface, Kieran was an average thirty-four-year-old bachelor who relocated to New Haven to start over. He lived in the small town in Terra for two years without incident.

Everyone knew him as a self-made millionaire who was gracious enough to invest in several businesses. That was where the Gnosis came in. The Earth magic was only performed by Beldames. Other forms consisted of Oris and Vudeux. The latter being the most dangerous for a Beldame to perform. Vudeux took away free will. Anyone desperate enough to invoke this spell had nothing to lose. All forms of Chaos Magic were dangerous in the wrong hands.

Tonight Kieran would take Jaxon's advice and live a little.

There's no harm in enjoying yourself.

The gorgeous blond on his arm was proof. Her blue eyes were full of hope for where the night may end. His boss also ordered him to blend or she would report back to the Tribunal explain his mission was a failure. And Kieran was no failure.

This brought him back to the woman sitting before him, a fake smile plastered on her face as she moved the hair behind each ear. Kieran wasn't normally a fan of blondes; he was always more of a brunette kind of guy. The darker the hair, the better. In truth, the darker the skin the better. One woman came to mind.

"I know right." The blonde giggled, pushing her hair back again to no avail as it fell back in place.

Shit, what was her name?

"And then I told her, 'I'm vegan!' Can you believe her," she scoffed, allowing the red liquid from her wine glass to stain her pink lips before her tongue darted out to erase all traces of the tart liquid.

"I can't," was Kieran's only response as he took a sip of his ice water.

"You don't want a real drink?" his date asked him for the third time.

"No, thank you. I have work in the morning." And he wasn't an idiot. Kieran could guess two reasons why Kim...or was it Alicia, was with him. Sex and money.

Besides, there was a bottle of Macallan that sat half-finished at home. He'd been using it to lull him into a dreamless slumber. He wouldn't need it tonight he thought as he looked at his date.

Kieran wished he remembered her name, but only one woman's name was on his mind. This date was another excuse to erase it from his mind, if only for the night.

London's face haunted him, her eyes as dark as a storm in the middle of the ocean. Each emotion was fueled by defiance, begging to be tamed. Her skin was as smooth as satin and dark as the midnight sky. Each inch rivaled the brilliance of stars that reflected behind her eyes.

Too bad she hated him.

"Kieran?"

"Hmm?"

"Did you want to get out of here?"

"Sure London." The words slipped out without a second thought. His eyes focused on the woman behind his date.

"Candy."

"What?" Kieran asked as his eyes moved back to the woman sitting with him.

"My name is Candy. You called me London."

Fuck.

"Of course. Candy." Like a stripper. How could he have forgotten that, especially given the clientele at the club tonight?

A part of him felt like an asshole, but in the back of his mind, he didn't care. He knew her type. Candy didn't accept his date because she wanted to get to know him. She saw dollar signs. She was someone who wore yoga pants for no reason and said things like, "Charge it!"

"Take me home."

"Of course, Candy," already forgetting her name as his eyes caught a glimpse of London taking an order.

The loud screech that left Candy's mouth resembled what he imagined a banshee would sound like, shrill and frightening. But as instructed, Kieran gathered his jacket and headed toward the exit.

The drive to Candy's condo wasn't far from Renegades, and a part of Kieran felt his night spiraling out of control. He needed to salvage some part of the evening if he didn't want to go home with blue balls. He didn't want an awkward conversation with Jaxon if he returned too soon.

His eyes darted toward Candy at each traffic light until he finally formulated an apology that he knew would make her melt.

"I'd say thanks for a lovely night, but . . . you know," she huffed.

"Wait, Candy."

"What?!"

With more confidence than he felt, Kieran took her hand in his and recited the apology he'd practiced in his head, "I'm sorry. I was an asshole, but I want you to know that's not who I am, and I hope you can forgive me."

Kieran waited a moment, holding his breath, until he saw Candy's frown turn back into a smile. He had her hook, line, and sinker.

"You really hurt my feelings."

He didn't give a fuck about her feelings, "And for that, I am sorry. Let me make it up to you."

"How?"

With a smirk, Kieran leaned forward and captured her lips between his teeth before deepening the kiss. His hand moved up to grab her throat lightly, eliciting a moan. He was hoping a girl named Candy would appreciate some light breath play. He had her right where he wanted.

He needed her to help erase London from his thoughts, even if it was for one night. She was everywhere, even when she was nowhere. Kieran's annoyance ramped up as her face popped up again, forcing him to pull away from his date.

"Fuck, I'm sorry, that was inappropriate. I should go before I make things worse."

"Actually," Candy paused, "Do you want to come in for a drink?"

Candy's voice was breathier than he remembered, "Only if you want me to."

"I want you to," she answered.

His plan worked.

Once inside her condo, Candy wasted little time throwing herself at Kieran, her hands tugging at his belt to free what lay beneath his expensive slacks. A giggle bubbled up and floated through the air, its sound falling on deaf ears as Kieran lifted his head and focused on the ceiling.

The cold air hit his member for a brief second before warmth enveloped it, a slow pop and then a soft suction mingled with the swirling of Candy's tongue. Inch by inch slipped between thin lips until it hit the back of her throat, before moving away and repeating the action. The repetitive movement of Candy's head created the best friction until he felt it. The sensation pulled at his groin and traveled to his stomach.

"Oh god," Kieran groaned, clamping his mouth shut before London's name tumbled out again.

His eyes opened to see Candy looking at him with lust and anticipation. He hadn't removed any clothing, and at that moment he wished he hadn't looked down.

"What the hell!"

That was what Kieran wanted to know too, as his dick quickly became limp.

"Really?"

"I'm sorry. This has never happened before."

"Was it something I did?"

"No! Of course not." It had everything to do with the fact she wasn't who he wanted to see naked.

"Why? Is it that girl? London?"

"I'm so sorry —"

"Fuck you! Get the fuck out!"

That was a fair reaction. Kieran hoped the palate cleanser would help erase London from his mind. Instead, he thought of how she would look on her knees. The quick pull of his zipper signaled the end of his date.

All in all, the evening was a failure. He still didn't get laid, and now he had stripper lipstick on his dick.

That bottle of Macallan was looking better by the second. He'd have to find another way to get London out of his system.

SIX

The ride home from Candy's was anything but peaceful. A storm raged on in Kieran the longer he sat in silence with his thoughts. The night edged closer to two o'clock, where he would lock himself inside of his huge house and ignore the world for one more night.

Peace had an expiration date when it came to London. In the short time, he had known her, Kieran learned nothing about her. No, that wasn't true. Kieran learned one important thing. London was a bona fide smart ass.

A chuckle slipped past his lips before he reminded himself that she hated him and he didn't need that kind of trouble in his life.

"Focus on the mission."

The only problem was he didn't know what the mission was. He was picked over hundreds of other candidates and no one from his leadership would offer him any explanation about what he was doing in Terra. And he hadn't thought to question them.

Yeah, the bottom of his favorite bottle of Macallan was looking real good.

"Julian."

"Yes, sir," a voice boomed from the ceiling.

"Can you call Mason and schedule a meeting for tomorrow?"

Kieran pulled open his fridge for a late-night snack. He hadn't gotten to eat since Stripper Candy had stopped any chance of them making it to the restaurant.

"Stripper Candy, I should probably stop calling her that."

"Probably." Someone laughed which only served to startle Kieran until he saw who spoke.

"Jesus! What are you doing here Doc?"

"I'm a bodyguard. I'm here to guard your body. And don't call me Doc."

Smart ass.

"It's almost three in the morning."

"Heard you wanted to meet with me," was the rebuttal.

"How? I just asked Julian to call you. Why are you in my house?"

Julian might be a great AI, but he wasn't that impressive.

"So, this Candy . . . is she an actual stripper?"

"No," Kieran would circle back to the question later he thought before finishing with, "but if you saw her you would understand why I made the connection."

That was a dick thing to say.

Instead of repenting for his callous thought, Kieran looked around for a glass. He would pair his Macallan with the mac and cheese.

"Want some?"

"Nah, I already ate, but thanks."

"Suit yourself." The amber liquid filled the glass placed to the left of the Tupperware container. Kieran watched Mason from the opposite side of the marble slab contemplating when to bring up his presence once more.

"Wait, is that just mac and cheese? Cold mac and cheese and bourbon? Is that all you're having?"

"I don't judge you, Mason." The words muffled as Kieran shoved a spoonful of the cheesy dish into her mouth.

"The hell you don't," was the response, entwined with a sarcastic chuckle.

"How long you been here, Doc?"

"Didn't you need something, Boss?" Mason threw out instead.

Kieran didn't know why Mason got so bent out of shape over the nickname. The only person he hadn't snapped at for calling him Doc, was the one person who made it her life's mission to avoid him.

"Besides, I heard about Renegades event coming up. Wanted to see if you needed additional help."

Yeah. Chastity was a sore spot for Mason.

"It was actually tonight. Been talking to Jaxon, huh?" Kieran shoveled another bite of macaroni in his mouth.

"No, but I have a few choice words for him, Boss."

"How about from here on out you just call me Kieran. No Boss shit for tonight, and I'll cool it with calling you Doc. Deal?"

"Sure . . . Boss," Mason smiled getting in one final jab.

Well, two could play that game.

"Speaking of Renegades, how's Belle, Doc?"

Silence pierced the air, followed by a fork shoveled into the cold macaroni.

"Really, Mason?"

"Fine. How do you feel about partnering with a Devereux?"

More mumbling followed suit as Mason scooped a larger portion of food into his mouth. Kieran allowed himself to look at his friend for the first time since he'd arrived. Mason Cross kept his hair short and always made sure to cover his tattoos while on the job, except the one on his neck.

Kieran speculated the reason Mason and Chastity never worked out was due to the color of his skin. Chastity Belle couldn't care less whether he was black or white, but her family did.

Mason wasn't a bad looking guy. He was the same height as Kieran, but it was obvious he hit the gym more. If he had to guess, Kieran would say he was ex-military. Mason never spoke about his past, and Kieran never asked him. It worked out well.

"It'll be fine. Georgia Rae Devereux may still have a controlling share of After Dark, but by the end of the meeting she'll be begging me to bail her out."

"That confident, huh?"

"You got that information I asked you for?"

"Yeah, it's on your desk."

"Then I'm that confident."

The dirt Mason dug up was enough to tell him Georgia Rae had dug herself into a hole with a lot of different investors. She needed Kieran's cash infusion to keep her afloat and bail her out. The sooner she realized it was better to hand over the reins, the better.

"Damn, that sounds cold-blooded, Boss."

"What'd we just talk about Mason?"

"I don't know, what?"

"I think I prefer Jackass," Kieran mumbled while watching Mason pull the container of macaroni toward himself.

"Don't worry about tomorrow. Devereux won't know what hit her. Before the night is over, she'll be eating out of the palm of your hand."

Kieran thought about Mason's words and decided that he was right. No matter the outcome, he would come out on top.

Whether Georgia Rae Devereux wanted to sell to him, After Dark Bar and Grill would merge with Renegades.

Georgia Rae Devereux prayed her plan wouldn't come back to bite her in the ass. She hadn't made it into the Tribunal's inner circle just to end up in a jail cell on Styxx. Her family managed to secure a spot with Terra for five generations. She wouldn't fuck it up by being stupid.

The other four seats belonged to Pyre, Cerbi, Koré, and a representative for Styxx. Pyre and Cerbi were the only dark horses she needed to worry about. If they got wind of her plans, she wouldn't have a chance to wish for jail. She'd already be dead.

Everything she saw from her floor-to-ceiling windows was all thanks to hard work and dedication.

All five acres of her property were surrounded by a stone wall that wrapped around every square foot. She had the best security that money could buy and an exit plan if there ever came a time to execute it. She had nothing to worry about, but that didn't stop her, nonetheless.

"Hello."

Georgia Rae hadn't realized she had followed through with calling.

"Tick Tock."

"Wes?"

"Who's asking?"

"That's not important." Anxiety gripped her and held on tight as she took a deep breath to stop the wavering of her words.

"Mrs. Devereux, I presume."

The words were a statement but held an air of inquisition.

"Do you know why I've called you tonight?"

"If I knew, do you think I would have answered my phone, Mrs. Devereux?"

"I called—"

"What I do know," the voice interrupted, "is that this number is for emergencies only. Is this an emergency, Mrs. Devereux?"

"Of sorts," Georgia Rae hated the way he said her name.

"There is only yes or no, and judging by your answer, I'm going to go with no."

"What defines an emergency to you?"

Georgia Rae spoke softly into the phone, her voice steady compared to the storm inside her. Her late husband Maxwell had always taught her never show her cards too soon. A woman of her stature never allowed anyone to see her frazzled. As the first African-American CFO in her family she was a force to be reckoned with.

"Let's hear what you have to say first, and I'll tell you if I think it is one."

The voice didn't sound amused. Instead, the man known as Wes, was indifferent and calm. His voice bordering on mechanical.

"I need you to move up the timeline."

"Do you now?"

A hint of amusement layered underneath the surface of his question. Georgia Rae hated the condescending tone of his words but knew to tread lightly.

"Is that possible," Georgia Rae inquired instead of taking the bait. She had heard rumors of this moment but never thought it was real. Now that it was within reach, there was no way she would let it slip away.

The sound of screaming cut into her thoughts followed by crying.

"Is—is that screaming?" Bile rose in her throat as she listened to a rapid succession of thuds. Georgia Rae didn't need an answer to her question, she already knew deep down what it was.

"We're not moving up the timeline, Mrs. Devereux. Just make sure you're ready when I call you. Same place as discussed previously, and don't even think of not showing. I know where you live and would love to hear what you sound like if you catch my drift."

More thuds and screams followed to make sure Georgia Rae understood.

"Of course," she almost stammered.

"Don't call this number again."

The silence indicated her mystery caller ended their conversation. Now all she needed to do was brief her daughter on the meeting with Kieran Alexander, and pray metaphorical blood wasn't shed.

SEVEN

"Lonny, peep this."

The deep baritone voice boomed from too many directions in the club. Its cadence was like smooth bourbon, in the sense that it left London feeling warm and tingly inside.

Heat rushed to her cheeks instantly when the description quickly morphed into an array of innuendos. Her tawny skin displayed a slight rosy tinge to them.

"Damn my imagination."

Thoughts of the amber liquid moving its way down her body tugged at her in all the right places. It just happened to be the wrong place to be having them.

Stained hands made their way between ebony curls tightening close to her scalp. The wild coif had started the day in pristine condition until the humidity of Terra had attacked it.

If she wasn't careful, London might fall into the trap hundreds of other women had found themselves.

A couple of soft-spoken words and a body that belonged in a museum helped weave a web of seduction. Add-in a perfectly timed crooked smile, and no warm-blooded woman stood a chance.

How did she find herself surrounded by such gorgeous men?

"Shit!"

The distinct intro of Simon's retro mix drifted through strategically placed speakers, followed by loud screeching and cursing. London's head turned in the direction of the familiar voice to find there was no one visible. London pushed down a chuckle moving toward the end of the open space.

"Simon?"

Like The Great and Powerful Oz, the same sultry voice boomed from above. "There is no one by that name here."

Nimble fingers turned the knob to the door leading to a small office. To her left, three televisions displayed different portions of what would be the dance floor lending a glow to the dark room.

"We are not playing this song tonight."

"Yes, we are."

"Did you okay it with Jaxon or Kieran?"

London moved one step closer to the table Simon sat behind. The computer screen opened to whatever expensive software the club owned. Even in the dark, he was breathtaking, brown hair cut short, each strand in agreement with the other. His head bent just enough to cast a dim glow across his face. A black button-down opened enough for a few tufts of hair to peek out. Sex on legs.

Now, here she was gawking at him like any other impressionable teenager. The only difference was she knew where to draw the line. Look don't touch.

Silence lingered longer than London anticipated until she finally cleared her throat and said, "Fine. How about something that doesn't make me want to kill myself."

"Hmmph."

"Perhaps something more upbeat, this generation wants to dance to."

Emerald eyes glanced up from beneath heavy lids for the first time since London had entered the small space. For a second, she thought Simon would address her statement. Instead, he smiled that crooked smile that made her heart skip a beat and then looked back at his computer screen.

"You don't know good music, Lonny," he spoke softly, his eyes never leaving the soft glow of his computer screen.

She didn't know when that had become the official name that everyone at Renegades called her, but she found that she didn't mind as much as she thought she would.

"Oh yeah."

71

"Yeah," he smiled again.

Damn him and his crooked smile. "Simon—"

"Come with me."

The sudden movement of a metal chair against concrete startled London. Her feet took two steps back on instinct against the man who now stalked toward her like prey. Her five-foot-three frame was dwarfed against Simon's six-foot stature.

"What are you doing?"

Panic laced London's voice when calloused hands gripped hers and quickly twirled her in a circle. A burst of laughter escaped, laced with a healthy dash of fear. "Dancing with a pretty girl."

"Smooth talker," London laughed again, allowing her eyes to close for a moment. The wind that touched her face was a nice change of pace. There wasn't much space for big moves with all of Jaxon's equipment, but that didn't stop Simon from doing one final spin.

"Oh my god." The words left London's mouth louder than she intended.

Instant regret filled her chest as her eyes met a blue glare. This expression was nothing like the one on Simon's face. This expression was a permanent fixture that never seemed to budge.

Even now, with her body pressed against taut muscles hidden by flimsy material, London knew she had royally fucked up.

"I see y'all are working hard."

If Simon's voice was like a glass of warm whiskey then Kieran's was like downing the entire bottle. The slight tingle London felt before was nothing in comparison to the throbbing between her legs now.

Kieran only touched her wrist, and she was practically soaking wet. What the hell was wrong with her?

"Sorry, Mr. Alexander."

"Kieran, my man!" Simon laughed before pulling his friend into a quick embrace.

On days like this, London wished her skin was like the night that cradled the world. Adrenaline pumped through her veins, the rat-a-tat-tat of her heart pulsating harder with each breath she took. Her only wish was that she didn't make a fool out of herself.

"We discussed this London. Call me Kieran."

Even his voice trumped Simon's, a small accent accompanied by a hint of disappointment, the worst of all the feelings to have. Hate, she could handle, but the disappointment was a different beast altogether.

"Sorry, Sir."

"Don't worry about it."

Was that a smile? It was there one moment and then gone the next.

"Did you say happy birthday to Lonny?"

London could have sworn her heart stopped in that instant. She couldn't see Kieran's expression, but the silence spoke volumes. "It's not—"

"I'm trying to convince her to come party with me. If you think you can handle it," Simon winked, signaling for London to play along.

"Simon, I don't —"

"Happy birthday, London."

Kieran's words echoed like a crescendo of thunder crashing into London's eardrums.

"Thanks," lie forgotten, London's eyes held Kieran's gaze.

"No problem."

"I was just helping Simon with song choices. He agreed not to play any of his retro songs" thankful the two men couldn't see her blushing.

"I did not," Simon's laugh drifted toward her, and for a moment she thought she saw Kieran clench his jaw.

"I'm sure he loved all the help."

Was that a hint of jealousy?

Maybe she could get him to warm up to her after all.

"Can I talk to Simon for a second?"

"Sure."

The tension suffocated London as her eyes shifted between both men.

"Alone."

"Oh, yeah. My bad," she gasped, walking quickly toward the exit. London knew she needed to set a plan in motion to gain Kieran's friendship.

Friends spilled secrets and did favors for each other. Since her Resurrection, London hadn't made any real friends, other than the guys at Renegades. She had met Chastity once, but she barely stepped foot inside and London never went to the Garden.

It didn't matter, because come hell or high water, London was going to gain Kieran's trust. She just hoped it didn't cost her everything in the end.

"What's up, Stone?"

Cocky. Kieran knew plenty of men just like him and none of them scared him. If he wasn't afraid to break the law he'd Collect his aura in the blink of an eye, but laws were there enforced for a reason.

"I just wanted to talk to you about flirting with employees."

"Employees?" Kieran could see the amusement painted all over Simon's face as he asked, "You mean Lonny?"

"Yes. I mean London."

Simon's emerald eyes glanced toward the closed door and then back to Kieran, before he began to laugh, "Are you serious?"

"Yes. If she feels you're harassing her, it could put us all in jeopardy."

"I don't think she believes I'm harassing her. If anything, I think she likes when I flirt."

"Well, I don't want to risk it. Consider this a verbal warning."

"You know what I think? I think you like her too. I'm not afraid of some friendly competition, Stone. May the best man win."

Kieran ignored Simon's outstretched hand and use of his middle name. Simon overheard Eve use it one time. It was one time too many. "You're being a real asshole right now."

"What?!" Simon's faux surprise only made Kieran want to punch him in the face. "Fine. If you don't like her, then you won't mind if I ask her out on a date, right?"

"What's your game, Monroe?"

"What's yours? Don't act like we don't see you staring at her when she's not looking. You practically undress her with your eyes whenever you think no one is watching."

"I don't know—"

"Before you deny it, don't."

The denial on the tip of Kieran's tongue quickly disappeared. It would have been a lie. Even though he was on an assignment it didn't mean he couldn't admire beauty when he saw it.

It wasn't unusual for a Collector to engage in a physical relationship with Undesirables. If Royals could do it, why couldn't they? But London wasn't an Undesirable, she was a Beldame and that was much more dangerous.

The intensity in Kieran's eyes matched Simon's. What did he care if the two of them dated? She wasn't his problem. She was his employee.

"How about you address me like I'm your damn boss?!"

Simon's hands moved up as if to say he was not a threat. "My bad, Mr. Alexander. But if it's all the same to you, I think I'll stick to the relationship London and I already have."

The tension was palpable between the two men until Kieran broke the silence with, "Don't say I didn't warn you."

"Don't worry, I'll make sure to keep any other flirting outside of work hours."

Kieran's eyes followed Simon as he opened the door and disappeared around the corner. He didn't care if Simon dated London. He just needed to say it a few more times until he believed it himself.

EIGHT

Kieran hadn't stepped inside Obsidian in four years. Not since he became a collector. He used his code to access the elevator with ease. It seemed not all things were erased during the Shift that wiped all mention of him away. The ride up to the fifth floor reminded him of the last night he had stepped foot inside. It was the night he was recruited within the Citadel.

The elevator doors opened to music blaring. Kieran would never understand how the music didn't reach the inside of the metal sarcophagus. The atmosphere screamed sex and something else he could never put his finger on. It was how he felt each time he brought a girl with him. This was Kieran's element and he was away for too long.

Black leather furniture lined the walls, strategically placed along the corridor leading to a singular door at the end. Each item doubled as an implement for pleasure or pain. Bodies writhed to the beat of the music pulsing through invisible speakers. The words spoke of torture and being a sucker for pain. Pain that Kieran craved to dole out. The type of pain that was followed by a jolt of pleasure. London's face making an appearance begging to be punished like a good girl.

The next beat picked up allowing the vibe to flow from mellow to dark and dangerous. The door inches from his body as he rapped his knuckles against the only red door in the dungeon.

"Enter."

Kieran moved inside the room to find Eve sitting in a chair that resembled a thirteenth century throne. The black and purple clashed with the scarlet door. "Come in and close the door, Stone."

The door closed with a silent click drowning out some of the music. Kieran hadn't seen Eve in person since he was recruited. All other correspondences were made over the telephone or computer. To be in the presence of Khaiv Rexton was a great honor among the Collector community. She was a representative of Cerbi who sat on the council for the Tribunal. Her opinion held great weight which made Kieran nervous. She didn't call upon anyone unless it was dire.

"Eve." The name was short and to the point, Kieran liked that.

"Take a seat."

Kieran's eyes moved to a bench shaped like a stick figured horse. He didn't want to do as he was directed, but he wasn't stupid enough to disobey. Many asses had been spanked across its purple leather; Kieran could feel it.

Adon forgive me.

His ass made contact finally, a smile planted firmly across Eve's face. She was enjoying this knowing his background. Kieran had never been dominated by a woman; he did the dominating.

"Comfortable."

"Never better."

"Good to hear. I've brought you here because something alarming has taken place and the Tribunal needs it handled quietly. Sooner rather than later. We have sat on this news for weeks deliberating."

"Anything to be of service."

"Five years ago a Shift was performed that altered the memories of every inhabitant of Chaos. The Tribunal within the Citadel was not affected nor did they know what transpired. It wasn't until three weeks ago that the Citadel was infiltrated."

"That's impossible," Kieran couldn't believe what Eve spoke of. The Citadel was impenetrable. No one got inside unless they knew where to look. It was the only Conduit in Chaos that led directly to the council members. Every old member had their memories of the door to it wiped by a Beldame in service to the Tribunal.

"She disguised herself as an inhabitant of Terra. There have been rumors and urban legends of what they could do, but we could never have foreseen this."

"They?"

"Eldites."

Impossible!

The word reverberated around in Kieran's head bouncing around making its way to his mouth. "That's impossible. Eldites were eradicated centuries ago. No one would be stupid enough to break law four. Not when it cost all parties involved."

"That is why we need this handled quietly. The woman in question has dark brown skin, curly hair and wields fire from nothing."

"That could be anyone, Eve. Chaos is a big place."

"She resides in Terra. That narrows it down for you. Look, I'm not saying it will be easy. Just keep an eye out and if you see anything suspicious report back to me."

"Yes, ma'am."

"Great. And Kieran," Eve paused for a second, a glint of amusement in her eyes before she finished with, "stay for a while and have some fun."

But there was no fun in doing a scene with a random woman. Not when the woman he really wanted to hear scream his name was off limits.

"Kieran!"

London's throat burned. There was a scratchiness that was soothed for only a moment as she swallowed down the bile that threatened to make its way to the surface. Nightmares plagued London's nights once her memories returned after her Resurrection. Her mother, Ruby, explained because she was of mixed bloodlines that it was rumored that the memory loss was a precaution. It was said to give the other pure bloods of Pyre time to make the death permanent.

Now she wasn't sure if what her mother said was the whole truth. Ruby admitted to playing a part in some of the memory loss herself. London suspected the nightmares correlated with the lost memories Rissa bricked up.

But maybe this wasn't a memory at all. It felt more like a premonition as London was engulfed in flames. Another person stood in the background watching the whole thing. This wasn't just Fenix gone awry. This felt like dying and it looked permanent.

A light sheen of sweat covered London's body, her comforter crumpled on the floor next to her. Her only warmth was a thin sheet clinging to her body as her head tossed and turned. Bits and pieces of the dream clung to her like napalm, seared into her memory.

One moment she was angry at her father, her tantrum reaching full throttle, and then the next thing she knew, Kieran stood before her. For a moment, London stared at him in confusion. Words were forgotten, stuck in her throat as she opened her mouth and quickly shut it.

Wake up, London.

"Where is my father?" She had so many questions for him, but Kieran wouldn't answer her. Why wouldn't he answer her?

Wake up.

Cobalt eyes were replaced by scarlet and burnt-orange flames, each one dancing around London until they formed a perfect circle. The inferno taunted her to touch it, practically begged to have her hand reach into its fiery cavern.

It knew a part of her was still afraid of the flames. It just didn't care. It was a fear that stayed with her from the age of sixteen. Since the day that she killed her father. Only he wasn't dead, and now she was going to use Kieran to flush him out.

London! Wake up!

His scream crashed into her, shattering the illusion she found herself stuck within. London's temple pounded against her skull, a headache tapping at the door begging to be let in. The beginning of a panic attack writhed just beneath the surface with each beat of her heart, waiting to be embraced, like an old friend.

For a moment, she forgot to breathe.

For a moment, London tried not to think of the life she lost when she started that fire.

"London?!"

"Mom," her voice was small, similar to when she thought a monster lie in wait within her closet. Only this time she was the monster she feared.

"London, it's okay. You were having a nightmare."

Copper eyes moved toward a photo placed beside her bed of a young Black gentleman in an expensive suit.

Gray strands of hair were strategically placed among ebony ones.

This picture reminded her of the biggest mistake. If it wasn't for her tantrum, there would have been no chain reaction forcing them to hide from the Tribunal.

"I'm okay."

"You didn't sound okay." The look on her mother's face let London know she had her doubts. Mother's intuition was a scary thing. London needed her to trust her now more than ever.

"I promise."

London couldn't tell her mother the truth. If she knew that a Collector was so close to them, she'd pack them up and go on the run. London couldn't allow that to happen, not when she could use him to find her father.

"I promise." Her voice was more confident than she felt. She had gotten good at lying. This wasn't something she was proud of. It was a skill that had aided her well in the past few months. If it weren't for the lies, she wouldn't have learned she could do Chaos Magic. She had already mastered Oris. The next would be Vudeux, a form of compulsion.

"London, if you need to talk—"

"I don't. I promise."

"Okay. . ." Ruby's voice was hesitant for a moment before she stood.

"Whatever you have going on, just be careful."

"I don't know what you're talking about."

"Sure, you don't," was the only reply before London gave her mother the fakest smile.

"Besides, what's the worst that could happen?"

There was a war coming to New Haven.

Footsteps echoed loudly through empty alleyways, moving undetectable. Police presence was in full force with the upcoming holiday, Adarai. Vandals had ramped up their presence. With the new mayor's initiative to clean up the streets and crack down on crime, it was nearly impossible to move unseen.

Wes passed three in the last hour. It wasn't until he passed the second officer that he realized something—he was invisible. The tattered clothing he wore was the perfect camouflage. This section of New Haven held most of the towns unhoused near the warehouse district. Most of the buildings remained empty after the market crashed, leaving a lot of hard-working men and women out of a job and therefore unhoused.

He still laughed at the word every time he heard it. Unhoused?

A bullshit way to look at the city's homeless problem. Just slap a pretty bow on it and call it a housing issue.

Steel-toed boots moved toward stairs that led to a subbasement below street level. Memories of the phone call from Devereux replayed as the metal door creaked open and a cacophony of sounds assaulted his ears.

Wes's eyes moved around the space. It was hours since he walked several miles. He was getting out of shape. One needed to be physically fit for the type of work he did. Being out of breath was not an option, and right now Wes was struggling to catch his.

The process of taking air in and forcing it from the body was almost like the game tug of war. Each team needed to win and yet, the game was never quite finished until someone finally fell. The inhale and exhale of breath in the winter air practically tightened the vice around his lungs.

Every breath he took felt like a needle prick buried beneath his chest, and yet he reveled in the feeling. He couldn't say the same thing for Dominique. Her breathing was erratic as tears streamed down her face. Wes brought her to the warehouse in the dead of night and left her there. He thought she would cooperate more, but two weeks later proved him wrong.

Her charcoal locks moved as air from the industrial fan picked up. Wes's fingers grazed her cheek until his palm cupped the nape of her neck. The warmth from his hand was a contrast to the coolness he felt.

"If I remove this, will you scream again?"

Tears cascaded from bloodshot eyes as the young woman shook her head violently. Coffee-stained skin, littered with different shades of purple and black disappeared under the dimly lit room.

"Scream and it'll be very bad for you. Do you understand?"

This time his only response was a small nod of the head.

"Good girl."

Calloused fingers slowly removed the gag that was placed securely between cracked lips. The intake of breath was followed by another. Each new breath was a reminder of his earlier thought until he heard more breaths in and no breaths out.

"No, no, don't hyperventilate, Dominique."

Wes towered over the young woman watching her body shake. His brown hair was wet in appearance screaming wash me.

"I'm not Dominique. Please, I'm not Dominique. My name is Shannon. I just want to go home."

"We will, but I told you, I just have to do this last job, and then I'm out . . . for good. I promise."

"Please. Please, I just want—"

"Why are you being such a bitch?! I've already explained what needs to happen. I'll do this last job and then we'll be set for life!"

"Please, if you could just listen to me—"

"No! You listen." Wes rushed to her side, his temper flaring for the first time since he had relocated Dominique to the warehouse.

He needed her to let him do his job and think, why wouldn't she let him think? Wes's eyes held a glint from the overhead lights that morphed his features from attractive surfer dude to the serial killer he was. Amber flecks swam in a sea of green. Dominique had always liked that about his eyes. She would love it again if he had anything to say about it.

The young woman quickly shut her mouth and nodded her head. Wes could see the fear that had once been laughter and joy. He hadn't meant to frighten her. She didn't listen sometimes, and that made him very angry. It wasn't her fault. She just needed to learn not to interrupt him while he talked. He told her that before but she always forgot.

The glint of metal redirected his gaze toward the silver around her wrist. Dominique tried to run when he told her his plan, just like last time. This time he made sure she was sleeping before he moved her.

"Are they too tight?"

"Please—"

"Are they, Dominique?"

"Yes...no," the woman changed her tune when she saw the look on his face. "They're . . . no . . . they're fine."

"Good," Wes whispered silently, the shrill sound of his alarm filling the space.

"Now, don't try anything, okay? I don't want to hurt you, Dominique, but I will. Do you understand?"

The nod of her head was the only thing that followed.

"Good girl." The smile Wes provided was authentic. He loved when she did what he said no questions asked.

"I have to go. I'll see you tonight, Dominique." His hands moved back to the gag around her neck. He had too much left to accomplish before he was free to leave with his prize.

"Please...My name is Shannon Wilson. Please, I'm not —"

The young woman began to cry again as the gag was replaced. Each sob fell on deaf ears as Wes moved toward the stairs to his left.

He refused to call her Shannon. Shannon died the moment she smiled at him. Wes just needed her to come to the same realization, he thought as the door closed behind him.

Georgia Rae Devereux might be the wealthiest woman this side of the Dorlorbra Bay, but if she double-crossed him, Wes wouldn't hesitate to do what was necessary. What good was a fortune if she was dead?

Arctic air rushed toward him as he emerged from the shadows to blend in with the rest of the invisible men and women of New Haven.

November 1st couldn't come soon enough.

NINE

London convinced Simon to update his music selection, but he still managed to sneak in a couple of his retro remixes. Kieran didn't know how she convinced him, but London, had gotten Simon to nix half of his old ass music. Music blared through the speakers as the crowd moved their body closer and closer to their partner.

That wasn't what caught Kieran's attention. It was the view of Simon flirting with London as she took orders. The bastard was really going to pursue her even after what he explained. Part of what Kieran said was obviously a load of crap, but Simon didn't know that. The two were going at it for hours, and Kieran's mood had only declined since his eyes locked on them.

He watched from Jaxon's stolen television screens as London made her way from table to table, a smile plastered to her face. Her body moved like the currents of a river, crashing into each note that drifted through the packed building. Waves of sweaty bodies electrified the air. Kieran had to admit that since London had started as their new waitress, Renegades was always packed.

Renegades didn't have a uniform for staff, but London had rallied the other girls and a few of the guys. Now each one wore a form-fitting white tank. The ladies wore blue jean bottoms that might as well be underwear, while the gentlemen wore jeans that framed their asses. It was a good idea. Everyone wanted a little eye candy with their alcohol.

Ripped fishnets covered London's legs as Kieran's eyes moved down to her red high tops. That was when he saw it. In large font on the front of her shirt, it read, "Lick, Swallow, Suck, Repeat" inside a shot glass. The Macallan that was meant to be savored was now on his shirt and the desk before him. The innuendo was obvious and anywhere else would have been inappropriate. It was perfect for Renegades.

The stark contrast of her white tank top against her Sienna skin pulled Kieran's eyes toward her bosom. Without hesitation, he used the zoom button to get a closer look. Even in the darkened club, Kieran could see the beads of sweat covering her body. His eyes focused on her chest as she erupted in a fit of laughter. What he wouldn't give to slowly travel between the peaks of her breast and disappear beneath the cotton material.

"Alexander."

"Fuck!" His hands moved to zoom out but all he managed to do was close the entire video. He had been caught being a perv, the same thing he had cautioned Simon against. Was he just as bad as Simon? The thought pissed him off. He was nothing like that asshat.

Smooth, Kieran.

"My bad, man."

"It's all good." Kieran's hand pressed a button to turn the screen back on. A sigh of relief escaped his body when he saw London was no longer on the screen.

"Whatcha doing?"

"Working."

"Uh-huh," he heard behind him, willing his erection to disappear before he turned toward Jaxon. "Not stalking an employee?"

Kieran's glare locked with Jaxon, confirming what he already knew. That bastard stood with his arms folded and his signature smirk. Someone needed to smack that smug look from his face, but it couldn't be Kieran. No, he wouldn't prove him right.

"Shouldn't you be out there?"

"I could ask you the same thing?" Jaxon shot back.

"Kinda packed out there. Someone should ensure things don't get out of hand using the eye in the sky." Kieran knew that answer was total bullshit. He was spying on London and was caught red-handed.

"I saw what you were checking out."

"We talked about that, remember? Not gonna happen."

Jaxon remained silent. Kieran watched as he tried and failed to stifle a chuckle. The man lived to be a pain in his ass, and Kieran didn't need his shit right now.

"It doesn't matter," Kieran continued as he addressed Jaxon's comment, "I'm staying away from her as much as possible."

Kieran watched as Jaxon's eyebrows went up.

"I'm not in the fucking mood Buchanan, so how about we change the subject."

"I'm still trying to figure out what the subject is, I haven't said anything about anyone other than you," Jaxon laughed.

"Get back to work," Kieran shot back, his anger growing at himself and Jaxon.

"Whatever you say." Jaxon laughed louder as he turned and walked out of his office.

Kieran finally allowed his body to relax as the door clicked shut. He needed to get his head back in the game. With the Devereux deal still looming over his head. Kieran didn't have time to be pining over anyone.

His thought was interrupted by the creaking of the door opening again. "Damn it, Buchanan, I'm not in the mood!"

"I hope I'm not interrupting."

He'd know that voice anywhere. It brought out a side of him that he missed. A side that he had buried years ago, and he wasn't looking to dig up.

"Actually, you are."

"I just need a moment, if that is okay," London continued closing the door behind her, the sound of music becoming muffled once more.

"It's not," Kieran knew he was being an asshole, but he didn't need this right now. He needed London to walk away or he might do something he would regret.

"What's your problem?"

"I don't have a problem Miss Reign." Agitation bubbled beneath the surface, bordering on anger as Kieran redirected his gaze to London's face. She was equally agitated from her expression.

"Bullshit!"

"We are not friends, Miss Reign. You don't get to come into my office and demand my time. That's not how this works."

"How does this work then?"

"If you'd like to arrange a meeting to speak with either myself or Jaxon, make an appointment."

"An appointment?"

"Yes. Now get back to work."

"Why don't you come make me, because I'm not leaving here without speaking with you."

Those words stirred something deep within Kieran. He didn't take London for a brat. He was sure she hadn't said the words to arouse him, but it didn't stop the stirring in his pants.

"Miss Reign—"

"Mr. Alexander," London countered moving toward his desk.

"What are you doing right now? This is highly unprofessional. I didn't think you were the type to throw it around. First Simon and now me—unless you are working your way through the club. If that's the case—"

Kieran hadn't expected her to hit him.

"How dare you?!"

The temperature in the room became increasingly warm as Kieran watched London's chest heave up and down before he smirked and said, "You hit like a girl."

This time when she swung, Kieran was expecting it. His hand caught her wrist with little effort pulling her body against his. Soft lips crashed down pushing hard against London's. The fullness was nothing like what he imagined.

Kieran felt the moment London's body stiffened against his. He knew he should let her go. Instead, his tongue lightly traced her lips silently demanding entry. Kieran thought she might hit him again until her body relaxed. Rough fingers traced the curves of her body until they traveled to her ass, pulling her into his rapidly growing erection.

A moan floated between them, barely audible to his ears.

Was that him or her? What was he doing?

The questions rushed in like floodwater, forcing him to end the kiss as abruptly as he had initiated it.

"What was that?" London whispered.

"That was a mistake."

A huge fucking mistake.

Kieran did his best to shut down any sign of emotion that crashed like waves underneath the surface.

"Right."

Silence stabbed at him; the imaginary knife buried in his gut as he watched her eyes harden once more.

"Those tables won't wait on themselves, Miss Reign," Kieran's voice was nonchalant once more. His eyes moved back to the security system willing her to leave; unable to sit in his current condition.

"God, I really hate you right now," London's voice was strained as her hand moved to her chest. The sound of wheezing came in spurts as Kieran redirected his gaze to her. Kieran watched as her body doubled over.

"London?"

"Fuck." The word was whispered but Kieran still heart it.

"Son of a bitch." Kieran watched as London dropped to a knee. "I think you're having a panic attack. I need you to take a few breaths with me."

"I am breathing." London's gasped, the sound becoming more erratic by the second.

"You're doing an awful job then," Kieran joked in his poor attempt to lighten the mood.

"Fuck you." There was the anger Kieran needed. He needed her to direct her energy anywhere but the attack. This might work.

"It hurts so bad," London bit out in an attempt to hide her pain. Copper eyes looked up at him with panic and then diverted toward the ground, "Not now."

Kieran's eyes followed London's gaze and froze.

Impossible.

London's hands glowed white as she flexed them open and closed. A ball of fire materializing, growing larger by the second. Kieran wasn't sure what to do next, but he knew one thing; if he didn't get her to calm the fuck down she might burn down the entire building.

"Forgive me," he whispered under his breath as he grabbed London's hair at the base of her skull and tugged.

"Fuck," she moaned, eyes opening to meet his.

"Breathe, damn it."

Heat like he never felt radiated from London's hands as orange ribbons twisted around his forearm. His lips crashed against London's once more with more force than before. Their warmth like nothing Kieran ever felt before. An inferno burning him to his core.

Electric tendrils wrapped around their bodies forcing her to respond to him. Kieran wasn't sure it would work, but then the warmth began to recede. The kiss ending sooner than he wanted, but at least he finally heard the steady cadence of London's breathing.

"You good?"

A nod was the only response he received as silence moved in from all sides. It didn't take long before he brought up the elephant in the room. "You're an Eldite."

"What?"

"How is that possible?"

Kieran's heart pounded fast threatening to explode from his chest. He needed answers sooner rather than later as he watched London try to escape.

"Not so fast!"

"I don't know what you mean. And I'd like to leave now."

"I don't fucking think so." The kid gloves were off, London needed to explain herself. Instead, a sharp pain moved from his groin, radiating towards his stomach.

Kieran wanted to keep his body upright but it fell like a tree in a forest. The only thing missing was the yell of "Timber!"

And just like that London was gone as his eyes closed to block out the pain that radiated through his body.

TEN

Welcome to the Holodeck.

London stared at those words for twenty minutes inside the crowded coffee shop. She berated herself for being reckless enough to be caught. The lie unraveled fast in the presence of Kieran. All it took was one kiss and a rejection and she allowed her life to fall directly into his hands.

If she had any brain cells left, she would get her ass up and get the fuck out of dodge. As far as anyone knew she had quit. It was a few days since she had gone into work. The leap wasn't too far from the assumption that she just bailed on everyone. She wasn't going back in to work. She was screwed.

Skipping town crossed her mind several times, but it disappeared just as quickly as it popped into her head. Running wouldn't do anything. If she didn't address this now, she would be running for the rest of her life.

"You're an Eldite."

The words replayed on a loop; each time more sinister than she remembered. She didn't know what she expected would happen, but it wasn't a surprise panic attack.

So when those words tumbled from his mouth, London did the only logical thing. She ran. Half of her expected a knock on her door that night. Expected there to be wrath like she never knew brought down upon her.

When nothing happened, relief set in, and London felt she could finally breathe. Then she received a text from a number she didn't recognize with an address, a date, and a time to meet. London knew who it was. She had no plans to go until she received a follow-up text that said, "Don't show up. I dare you."

Her mother would call her a fool for showing up. She would have already been two states away had she known what had transpired. It was obviously a trap. But London didn't want to see what happened if she ghosted him. She didn't know what pull he had beyond Renegades. He was obviously someone who knew about the lore.

Now she waited at the appointed time inside a coffee shop named Beam Me Up Java Co., and Kieran was twenty minutes late.

"Fuck this."

With confidence she didn't possess and a renewed anger, London walked toward the exit stopping short of the door. There stood Kieran with a look she couldn't quite place. He wore jeans and a t-shirt like the first time she saw him. Under any other circumstances she would find him attractive. Sexy, even.

"Leaving so soon?"

But at the present time, she wanted to punch him in the face.

"Of course not."

The red tee hugged Kieran's chest, which London found ironic. She could only see red at the moment herself. With one step back, she watched Kieran's eyes travel down her body and back up to her face. She knew better than to get too close.

His expression was unreadable, a look she saw before. This was different than lust. She had seen lust before, this was something much more sinister. Much more animalistic.

"After you."

London cursed herself for not being fast enough. If she played the situation smarter maybe she could have drawn out this meeting. There was no use in thinking about what ifs now as she took steps toward the furthest table.

"Thank you for meeting me," Kieran spoke after he sat down across from her.

"Not like I had a choice."

"You always have a choice, Miss Reign."

Miss Reign?

So formal for someone who held her life in the palm of his hand. He could call her anything that he wanted. He could turn her in and wash his hands of the situation. So why didn't he?

"Show or go on the run. Seems like shitty choices if you ask me.

London saw Kieran's jaw tightened at her choice of words. Did he not like them? To fucking bad.

"Shitty choices or not, they were yours to make." When London didn't respond he continued with, "You must have a death wish. You've been working at the club for weeks."

"What can I say? I like to live life on the edge."

London knew she should dial back the sarcasm. She knew that she was poking the bear and yet, she couldn't put her stick away to save her life. Her mouth and brain were no longer connected. Part of her knew her fate was sealed as she leaned back with her arms crossed, waiting for what came next.

"How did you hide your true aura?"

"I didn't."

"So you have help."

London remained quiet. If there was one thing she wasn't it was a snitch. Especially not to a Collector who could report them all to the Tribunal and have them carted off to Styxx.

Law four.

Or worse.

"Are you responsible for the recent Shift?"

"Are you going to turn me in?" London countered. She had a million questions of her own. She didn't have time to answer things that didn't matter. Whether she knew about the Shift or not wasn't important at the moment. Her life hung in the balance and that took precedent for her.

"That depends," Kieran responded, matching her body language with his hands crossed across his muscled chest.

"On what?"

"Do you know what I am?"

"A giant asshole?"

"Language. You know what I mean."

London did indeed know what he meant. Her only cue was a slight nod of the head. She couldn't bring herself to say it out loud. It sounded crazy when she said it out loud.

"There has to be a reason you've stuck around for this long."

"You're right. There is."

London didn't volunteer more information. The less she said, the better, at this point. She had to think of her mother in all of this. Ruby warned her, but she didn't listen.

The sound of tapping returned London's attention back to Kieran. Her eyes shifted toward the blue pools.

"You gotta give me something here."

"To crucify me? Pass."

"No one is crucifying you. Yet."

Doubling down, London asked, "What do you want to know about me? About my bloodline?"

"That'd be an excellent start. If you are what I think then I know you are dangerous. The offspring of a

Highborne and Collector. Your kind is easily corrupted by the power you wield."

"Do you think I wield much power?" London shot back knowing that her eyes were just as marigold as her mother's sometimes turned.

"You infiltrated the Citadel. So, I would say yes. You wield too much power."

"I've never been in the Citadel. I wouldn't even know how to find it."

"That's not what my boss told me.,"

"Well your boss is wrong."

"Eve is never wrong about matters such as this."

"Eve? The darkness is your boss?"

"If you didn't mean to sneak into the most secure building in all of Chaos then you're unpredictable. That's just as bad."

"Absolute power corrupts absolutely, is that it?"

"Exactly."

"You're wrong."

"Am I? The only thing I can't figure out is how you flew under the radar for so long. Even as I sit here, I see your aura. It's like every other Undesirable in Terra. If you aren't a Beldame, how is that possible? Unless, you have a Beldame in your pocket. Is that it?"

"I will give you answers if you help me," London answered ignoring being called an Undesirable.

"Help you?" The incredulous grunt escaped Kieran's mouth making London almost flinch.

Almost.

Holding her composure, she offered, "My goal wasn't some kind of coupe. The goal was to eventually get close enough to you so that I could find information on my father."

"Your father."

"Yes. A Collector—like yourself," London added.

"Your mother is the Highborne. Of course. Why didn't I put it together. You're the family of Jacqueline Reign. Holy shit!"

"Keep your voice down." London's eyes moved to each patron to find no one had noticed Kieran's outburst.

"Why do you want to find your father? He's safer wherever he is."

"Debatable."

"And who is your father?"

"I will tell you once I'm sure you won't turn us in to the Tribunal."

After a long pause, Kieran placed his forearms on the table and leaned in. "I'm not going to turn you into the Tribunal. And I'll help you track down your father."

It was her turn to pause and think about his words. She didn't have any other choice but to consider his offer.

"What's the catch?"

There was always a catch.

"When you spiraled at the club, do you remember how I got you to calm down?"

London turned her gaze away from Kieran, the memory of his lips on hers causing her body to heat up. "Vaguely."

"I want to explore that dynamic."

"How do you mean?"

"I'd like you to allow me to teach you to control your abilities. My methods of discipline will be a bit— unorthodox."

That didn't answer London's question. It also didn't explain why he would want to help her when it would make him an accessory.

"You'd also be required to move into my home while this training takes place."

There was the catch.

"I'm not doing that."

"If you want to find your father and stay hidden you will."

"You're blackmailing me? What happened to you not turning me into the Tribunal."

"Blackmail sounds almost criminal. Consider this a business venture. I have something you need. In return, you will abide by some rules to help you control your impulses."

"My impulses are fine."

Without missing a beat Kieran leaned forwards and whispered, "That's not what the Tribunal thinks."

His body language never changed as he leaned back moving his eyes up and down London's body. She didn't know what Kieran's end game was, but there was no way he thought she would take him at his word so easily. He must want something else.

"I'm not sleeping with you, if that's what you're aiming for. I'm not that kind of person. I'm not a slut or whore…or whatever you think."

"Sex is not required, but it can also be negotiated. If you'd like," Kieran smirked.

"Negotiate? Is that what we're doing right now because it feels like you have my life in the palm of your hands."

"The only other option is you have is leave town, and I don't help you find your father. Your choice."

Anger bubbled beneath the surface, threatening to boil over until Kieran whispered, "I'd put a lid on that if I were you."

London's eyes moved toward her hand. The glow quickly gone once she got her breathing under control. Kieran was right. She couldn't afford to keep allowing her emotions to run unchecked. She needed to learn to control her abilities. There was a part of her bloodline that she didn't understand. As a Highborne she knew that she could tap into her ability Fenix, and with just enough of a push she could control fire elements.

As a Collector, she was lost.

"Fine."

"Fine?"

"Yes, you bastard. Fine," London hissed through clenched teeth.

"Perfect. And since you love to lie, we will start your training on your actual birthday. That's Adarai, right?"

Adarai's date changed every year but is always the last Saturday of October. Its tradition is drenched with mythical roots associated with coming-of-age rituals, night walks, scavenger hunts and costumed mascots. Children and adults alike adorn costumes of different mascots and celebrate the ancient holiday. Officially celebrated for one day, the festive atmosphere was already in the works.

"That's in two weeks! And I didn't lie. Simon did."

"You didn't correct him though did you?"

"But—"

"Work will go on as usual. As far as anyone knows, you've been sick. I'll have my guest house ready up for you."

Words eluded London at this point. She was making a deal with the devil.

"Any questions for me now?"

"No."

"Sir," Kieran added.

"What?"

"From now on, you are to end your responses with the word Sir. No, Sir. Yes, Sir. Please, Sir," Kieran smirked, she could tell he was loving the mix of anger and embarrassment that radiated from her.

"No—Sir," London forced out, hands clenched into fists.

"That's better Sam."

"Sam? Do I not get my own name either?"

"It's not meant to be a name, not in the sense you are thinking."

"What is it if not a name?"

"Welcome to Beam Me Up, can I get you started with our Spock-a-licious Americano?"

London cursed the intrusion. They had been sitting secluded for some time, and now the barista decided to come to check on them. Did they do that at coffee shops? London's eyes shifted to the rag clenched in the young girl's hands and the bottle of cleaning supplies nearby.

"No thank you, I'm actually leaving," Kieran rose from his seat. "Save the number from this morning."

"Aye aye, Sir," London answered with a salute.

"See you at work, Sam," Kieran smirked with a nod to the barista before he made his way toward the exit.

It was at that moment that London realized her mother was right. She needed to be careful, now more than ever.

ELEVEN

If the overcast skies were any indication, of what was to come, then Georgia Rae was screwed. She kept her word and refrained from calling Wes back or as she begun to call him, "Mr. W."

Georgia Rae felt calling someone she knew was a career criminal by his first name made the circumstances more tangible. And if there was one thing she learned from watching hours of crime shows, it was that she needed plausible deniability.

The only sound that accompanied Georgia Rae's thoughts was the slowly ticking of her blinker waiting at the traffic light near the Grand Parkway. She had exactly one block to figure out a game plan if she wanted to save her bar, and Georgia Rae knew that was not enough time.

Even as she turned into the damaged parking lot she knew her time was officially up. With each pothole her tires sank into, Georgia Rae felt a little bit of her resolve disappear. After Dark Bar and Grill had been the brainchild of her late husband, and letting it fail felt like she was spitting on his memory.

Now she sat on the wrong side of the tracks in a strip mall that ironically had a strip club, nestled between Renegades and a craft superstore. Georgia Rae didn't like to announce she was better than other people, but she was better than this. She didn't need a meeting to tell her she could never allow her name to be associated with an establishment like Renegades.

Louboutin heels touched shattered pavement, the perfect metaphor for everything in Georgia Rae's life. Each click, a nail hammered deeper into her metaphorical coffin because if she agreed to their terms she'd be the laughingstock of New Haven for sure.

Music filled the space as Georgia Rae stepped inside the empty club. Her eyes slowly drifted from one end of the club and stopped on the incredibly long bar. Glass bottles glowed from the ambient lighting that was expertly placed behind each one as the color shifted from neon green to a vibrant blue.

It didn't escape Georgia Rae's attention that Renegade's color scheme was similar to After Dark's. Splashes of scarlet and onyx were interwoven among autographed images of celebrities and rusted metal.

The vibe screamed biker bar to the far left with the presence of pool tables and dart boards. But as her eyes fixated on the center of the room she was drawn to an obvious booth, and a large sign that spelled out Renegades in chunky letters.

Georgia Rae could see the appeal once she stepped inside, but just as she thought, it was a little too rough around the edges for her. After Dark's clientele had a certain sophistication she didn't feel Renegades possessed. Even her body language screamed she didn't belong and if she didn't belong then the 1 percent who frequented her establishment certainly wouldn't fit in either.

Five generations of Devereux's had lived in New Haven for as long as Georgia Rae could remember, which at the time was rare. Black families didn't mingle with their white counterparts. It was unheard of to have a Black family on the same block. But that didn't stop Lillian Devereux from moving her family to the most affluent part of town and making a name for herself.

Her great-grandmother's decision to invest all her money in a rundown bar on faith and prayer paid off in the long run. Lillian Devereux was the reason Georgia Rae could afford to wear the expensive designer clothing that formed snuggly against her body.

Manicured hands smothered down her pencil skirt, almost afraid something would come from nowhere and stain the fifteen-hundred-dollar outfit.

Georgia Rae's mind was made up. She would hear out the owners and respectfully decline their offer.

"Hi. Sorry, we're closed."

Georgia Rae's amber eyes traveled to the tall gentleman standing near the booth. She had been so engrossed in her memory she hadn't heard him sneak up on her. His dark jeans and dingy t-shirt reminded Georgia Rae of a mechanic or better yet a biker working on his most prized possession.

"So, this is Renegades," Georgia Rae announced while doing her best to avoid moving from the spot she allotted herself. Her eyes briefly left the emerald stare of the stranger before her. His dark brown hair was as disheveled as the clothing he wore.

"It is."

Short and to the point. She liked that. Georgia Rae hadn't expected someone as handsome to work in a club like Renegades. He could easily belong to her 1 percent. And if he didn't he would fit in beautifully.

Music was the only thing that hung in the air between the two of them until he repeated, "We are closed though. We open again at five for our happy hour. You should check us out then."

There was that smile she imagined. It was award-winning and swoon worthy. However, today was not the place, nor the time to allow fantasies to take over. Georgia Rae cleared her throat and confidently announced, "I'm aware. I have a meeting with the owners."

Her tone was condescending, and as much as she knew she should care, Georgia Rae did not.

"Of course, you must be Mrs. Devereux. My apologies. Jaxon is expecting you, please follow me."

Georgia Rae allowed her feet to move toward the ruggedly handsome man. His ass was firm enough to bounce a quarter off just like the saying said. Maybe she could allow herself to fantasize just a little.

The click-clack of her five-inch stiletto heels echoed through the space. The young man took her down a corridor and stopped outside a scarlet door, the same color scheme as the club and Georgia Rae's outfit.

Red was thought to be inappropriate when interviewing, muted colors were always preferred. Georgia Rae didn't want the owners of Renegade to look at her and think of the word tame. No, she wanted them to look at her and realize she was a force to be reckoned with.

"If you need anything feel free to holler. Just ask for Simon"

Finally, a name to go along with the handsome face as he knocked twice on the crimson door and opened it. Georgia Rae wasn't sure what she would find behind the closed door, but what she was not expecting was how sophisticated it looked compared to the main aesthetic of the club.

Georgia Rae's eyes moved to the built-in security system surrounded by white wooden shelves. By appearance alone, it looked to be much more technologically advanced than she would have expected for the rustic nightclub. Coupled with the small, half-rounded windows on either side of the room and Georgia Rae had to admit she was impressed.

"Jax, your guest is here."

"Thanks, Simon. I'll take it from here."

"You got it," Simon nodded before closing the door behind him.

"It's a pleasure to finally meet you Mrs. Devereux," Jaxon offered a small gesture toward one of the large chairs across from him.

"Please, call me Georgia Rae," she replied instead, a faux smile plastered on her face.

"Of course, we here at Renegades—"

"Sorry to interrupt, but speaking of we, I thought there was another owner," Georgia Rae commented when she only saw one individual inside the office.

"There are two owners, you are correct. Mr. Alexander had an emergency and apologizes for his absence."

"Something more important than the fate of my business," the irritation was evident in Georgia Rae's voice as she allowed her ego to surface.

"I assure you he knows the importance of a businesswoman's time such as yourself. I didn't feel there was a need to reschedule. I hope that is okay."

"It's not ideal, but I'm here. You have ten minutes to wow me Mr. Buchanan."

"I'll take every second because that is how amazing we believe we could be."

"I'll be the judge of that."

"We are prepared to off you a generous amount to sell After Dark. You would retain royalties from bar sales of course and be paid a salary to continue being the face of the brand. What do you think?"

Georgia Rae thought he was out of his ever-loving mind if they expected her to make a deal as asinine as selling her shares to them. Instead, what she said was,

"Royalties and a salary? I was under the impression that you would be offering a partnership, not a coup."

"It is not our intention to make you feel misled, but this offer could help alleviate your debt problem and put money in your pocket."

"Mr. Buchanan, this isn't a negotiation. I wanted to see what I would gain from attaching my family's name to your establishment. I came. I saw. I am not impressed," Georgia Rae fired back.

"Georgia Rae—"

"That's Mrs. Devereux to you."

"Everything is a negotiation, Mrs. Devereux."

The energy in the room was supercharged as Georgia Rae tried her best to keep a cool head.

"Not this, Mr. Buchanan," Georgia Rae finally announced as she stood from her comfy seat and turned on her heels to storm out of the room. Hell would freeze over before she ever sold After Dark.

London sat in parking lot and contemplated just turning on her car and taking the option that had her getting the fuck out of dodge. Memorial Park was nestled near the outskirts of town but close enough to be where all the soccer moms went to watch their kids play on a Saturday afternoon.

When she had saved Kieran's number she hadn't expected him to text her or even call until she had to move into her state-of-the-art prison. It had been less than three days and he was already calling her to meet him in the park.

It was hell lying to her mother, but what she didn't know wouldn't hurt her. If she knew what was happening she would take option two and flee, but finding her father was too important to let the opportunity pass her by.

Now she sat in the parking lot waiting on Kieran once again. Maybe she was crazy after all to think it was a good idea to—

"Jesus!"

The tap on her window had London's heart racing like a horse on meth. Or what she imagined a horse on meth to feel like. She knew the imagery made no sense. Just like it made no sense to see Kieran's stoic face mouthing for her to get out.

"You scared the shit out of me!"

"You should pay more attention to your surroundings, Reign."

"Are you gonna start calling me by my last name too?"

"I'd call you by your middle name but I don't know it," the smart-ass comment whipped out faster than London could say go.

"What does that even mean?"

Exasperation filled every syllable that came from her mouth.

What was she doing with him?

Why was he being so cryptic?

And why was he leading her toward an expensive vehicle?

"Get in."

"Pass."

"It's not a request. Get in, Reign."

"I'd prefer if you called me London. How do I know you aren't going to take me to the Tribunal as soon as I'm in the car?"

"Because I made you a deal and I always keep my word."

When London didn't respond, Kieran continued by saying, "I didn't think you would come. I thought maybe you took option two and ran. I see you keep your word as well."

"Fine. I'll go, but just know I'm not afraid to claw your eyes out if I need to."

"Noted. Get in."

The drive to Kieran's home was unfamiliar as they rounded a corner to a house that sat looking over the rest of the town. The rest of the houses below were ants in comparison to the full-blown mansion London was looking at.

"Figures."

"Do you ever shut up, Reign?"

This time London almost smiled at the sound of his irritation. Why did that make her happy? It was obvious that she had struck a chord and yet it didn't bother her one bit. If anything, it lit a small fire under her she didn't even know existed.

Once inside, London realized it lacked that feminine touch. Everything was white with a touch of onyx and gold.

"You don't have any photos or paintings up."

It wasn't a question. London just found it odd as she turned her back to him for the first time since meeting him in the park.

"There are albums somewhere."

"How old are you?"

"I'm thirty-four, a few years older than you. Why?"

"Curious, I guess."

"You know what they say about curiosity."

"Yeah, well—"

"What do you want for your birthday, Reign?"

Kieran's breath cascaded down her neck as his body moved closer to hers. His fingers touched her arms sending heat up her body. Electricity coursed through her as the air became humid. London's breath hitched as she turned toward him.

"I want to find my father."

Cobalt eyes looked down into her copper ones as they flickered marigold.

Did he have to be so close?

London moved her head to look away from him, anything to break whatever hold he had on her. When she felt the heat of his breath on her neck she stifled a moan that threatened to escape.

Soft lips made contact with the base of her throat, slowly moving up toward her ear, "You need to control your emotions."

"I—"

"I've got a lot to explain about your bloodline. But I need you to trust me."

"I don't trust anyone right now," London answered pushing her body away from his. She needed whatever emotions he pulled from her to settle down. Emotions were what got her in this predicament. If she had practiced more before jumping in feet first things would be different. Instead, she stood in the enemy's living room listening to him ask her to trust him.

"I don't trust anyone," London repeated.

After a brief second, Kieran nodded his head and said the one thing she wasn't expecting.

"Good."

TWELVE

"The first thing that all newbies learn is how to harness the ability of Sight."

Kieran had never been someone's mentor before. He was recruited at the age of twenty-nine himself. Being a Collector was new for him. The difference between the two was he had chosen this life and London had unfortunately been born into it without any instruction.

Add the fact she was also an Eldite and it added an entirely new level of complications no one prepared anyone for. Archives about Eldites remained sealed. Most had been lost centuries before he was even a name in the wind. Asking about them would send up alarms Kieran didn't need. He'd need to do this himself with what information he had and pray she knew something of her Highborne lineage.

If not, they were both at square one.

"To tap into your Sight, you must remove all distractions, both mentally and physically. It takes a lot of concentration at first, but once you do it enough it becomes second nature."

"Sight? Like premonitions?"

"Not quite. Every soul has an aura attached to it."

"Like those hokey psychics who say they can read auras?"

"No." The throbbing at the base of his head was starting to grow. Why couldn't she just listen to him for once and not act like a brat.

"What do they look like?"

"It's not only what you see, but it's also what you feel too. Although visual auras are the most common of the two, it is also possible to feel someone's aura as well."

"My mom never mentioned anything about auras."

"Maybe she didn't know. Collectors and Highborne are alike in the fact that we can use the electricity around us to convert it into energy. For you it's fire and for Collectors, it is a faint color that surrounds every individual, whether they be Collectors, Highborne, or Undesirables."

"I see." London turned her head away at the mention of Undesirables. For years she had thought of herself as an Undesirable. The word held negative connotations for her even if she knew she was technically of royal blood lineage.

"Centuries ago, the Tribunal decided that each soul would have a specific color assigned depending on the province they lived."

"Terra is green," London added, letting Kieran know that she was listening. Her head turned to face him and for a moment he wanted to praise her. But only for a moment.

"Correct, it is where all Undesirables are housed."

"And what color is Cerbi?"

"Cerbi is black. It's where all Collectors reside."

"Do other species—is that correct? Species? Do they live in each province?"

"The correct word you are looking for is class and no," was the only response Kieran provided.

"So it's segregated. Why not try to bring everyone together?"

"That's not how it works beyond the Veil."

"Maybe someone should fix that," London offered.

"Why fix what isn't broken?" Kieran countered.

"Who says it isn't broken."

"One lesson and you think you know so much, huh?"

Kieran could see London wanted to make a snarky remark. He watched her muscles tense and then slowly relax. There was that pride again.

She was learning it wasn't always best to mouth off. There was a benefit to listening and that would factor into their lessons if she allowed them to continue.

"It's not our job to question the order of things, Reign."

"What is our job, then Stone?"

Kieran was caught off guard by his middle name. Collectors were able to pick the name they wanted once they were recruited.

Cerbi was the only province beyond the Veil where the Tribunal convened. It served to hold council and guarded the other provinces against those who might find their way through a Conduit from Terra.

It was rare, but it wasn't impossible. London was a prime example of making the impossible happen.

"Our job is to make transitioning from your every day life a little less scary. Entering the Veil is not a death sentence, but it is permanent. And Undesirables have proven the most unpredictable when Collected."

It wasn't lost on Kieran each time he said the word Undesirable, London's body stiffened. It wasn't a noticeable reaction. But as soon as the word passed his lips, Kieran could see London's jaw clench tight. She wanted to say something.

"Do you not like the name?"

"I do not," was all London said.

"Why?"

Kieran watched London's bottom lip become trapped between her teeth. He gave her his a list of dos and don'ts before their lesson began. One of the don'ts was to cool her snarkiness. He didn't realize it would hurt her so much, but he did derive joy from it.

"All my life I believed I was half Human. Undesirable," London's voice broke through his thoughts like a child carefully choosing her words.

"I know what you're thinking. I was also half Highborne. As a female that doesn't make me a Battleborne. Only men are considered soldiers and women are branded Undesirable. Do you know who wants to Contract with an Undesirable? No one."

"I suppose not," was all Kieran voiced.

"When you know the world holds wonders you could never expect, and of all the wonders it doesn't want you—" Her words cut off with the swipe of a hand to her face.

Was she crying?

As much joy as he got from knocking her down a peg, seeing her cry pulled at him in a way it never had before. Everything about London pulled at him differently. Kieran wasn't born a Collector, he was chosen. His ability to keep calm in dicey situations, and his ability to think on his feet, were praised. Emotions hardly ever factored into what he did.

Instead, he found himself saying, "Fair enough. We'll stick with the word Human for now. But London even if you were half Human you could never be an Undesirable."

Kieran received a nod from London, before her face became a brick wall and her back straightened. He needed to stop the sappy bullshit and get back to business.

"Close your eyes, Reign."

Kieran almost smiled at the look London threw his way. She meant it when she told him that she didn't trust anyone, but for this to work he needed her to let go of that mistrust for just a moment. Collectors needed to trust each other to some degree.

"Just this once, trust me."

After a moment, Kieran watched as London closed her eyes but her body was still tense as if she was waiting for someone to attack her.

"Breathe in your nose and out your mouth. Yeah, just like that. Breathe in. Breathe out."

Kieran's eyes moved to London's chest, the slow inhale and exhale of her breath caused her chest to move up and down slightly.

"Is this necessary?"

"Yes. Keep your eyes closed and tell me what you feel."

"Nothing," was London's immediate response.

"You aren't trying, London," Kieran shot back using her first name for the first time since he found out about her secret. She would need all the concentration in the world if she wanted to find her father. A Collector was hard to see unless you were one as well. One that went into hiding would be hell to find because he could easily pay to have his aura changed. Their were still ways to figure out their true nature, Kieran would get to that later.

"I don't feel anything, Kieran." The exasperation evident as she opened her eyes and crossed her arms across her heaving chest.

"You want to find your father, correct?"

"Of course."

"Then close your eyes and listen to the sound of my voice."

Kieran watched as London closed her eyes once more. If he wanted her to experience Sight, he'd have to let down some of his walls and let her in as well. That was how it worked. Undesirables—Humans, didn't know they were essentially being stalked like prey. And because they don't know they go about life with their guards completely down.

"Now, listen to my voice. Listen to the cadence of each word as it reaches your ears. Do you feel that?"

"Yes."

"Good. Now take a deep breath and imagine what I look like. From my hair to my shoes—you see me."

A breathy sigh escaped London's mouth before Kieran heard her say, "Yes."

"Now open your eyes, but don't focus on my features. Focus on the things you normally can't see. Focus on the vibrations that your body feels right now. Focus on the way my breathing moves my body, the way I move. Can you do that?"

"I—I don't—" London began until Kieran whispered near her ear.

"I believe in you, Sam."

Kieran watched London's eyes open to tell him off but the words never left her lips. Her expression was pure shock. "I see you."

"What do you see?"

"Static. Waves that move like the vibrations you mention. It's—holy shit. It's amazing."

"It is. Now I want you to close your eyes and push the energy down with your mind."

"How?"

"Visualize it as a tangible object and place your hands above it. Once you can see that, I want you to press down as hard as you can mentally and then open your eyes again."

Silence filled the space until Kieran watched London's copper eyes open and a smile spread across her face. "I did it," she whispered to herself in disbelief."

"Good job, Reign."

"Thank you."

"Don't thank me just yet," Kieran began before he moved closer to her, circling her until his check pushed against her back. "Tit for tat, Reign. I showed you something and now I need something from you."

"I told you; I'm not having sex—"

"I need a name." Kieran cut London off before she embarrassed herself more than she already had.

"A name?"

"Specifically your father's name."

Kieran expected there to be hesitation on London's part. After all, he was asking her to give up her Creator's name. She knew about Vlosyrós Law. Smart girl.

"No name, no Collector. That's how most investigations work, London or do you still think I'm going to turn you in."

"You're right," he heard London blow out a breath of air she had been holding, "The plan was to gain your trust first, but I need to know. My memories are vague, but I do remember my mom calling him by a weird nickname as a child."

"Weird, how?"

"It might have only been weird to me," London backpedaled.

"What did your mom call your father?"

There was more silence between the two before she announced, "Diablo."

No. It couldn't be.

Kieran only heard one other person use that moniker. And it was impossible he wouldn't know this vital part of his life. Even now he could see his face and hear his words of wisdom.

"London? Is your father, Lucas St. Claire?"

"Yeah. How did you know that?"

Kieran knew because Lucas St. Claire, also known as Diablo in Cerbi, had recruited him. He was the reason Kieran became a Collector.

The man he held in high esteem was the very man that could pull his world down on top of his head.

"We got a lot to talk about."

THIRTEEN

Denial, anger, bargaining, depression, acceptance. The five stages of grief. London read somewhere that psychologists believed everyone went through all five stages eventually in their own time.

Your father is my mentor.

The words bounced around London's head like a marble ricocheting off of every surface of her brain. Even now she couldn't process the words that came out of Kieran's mouth.

Your father is my mentor.

Obviously, it was a lie. Her father wouldn't essentially start a new family and just leave her to rot. Would he? Kieran's shocked expression told London everything she needed to know. Her father had fucking continued on with his life as if he didn't have a wife and kid that could die at any second. Lucas St. Claire was living his best life free of any entanglements.

Maybe if she could talk some sense into him. He wouldn't let his only child die. London's last thought multiplied into one after another until she had an entire fake life figured out in her head.

What if she wasn't the only child?

The fourth level of grief set in fast as she thought of how in a way Kieran was like a son to him, although he wasn't a blood relative. Her father had taught him the things she struggled with on a day-to-day basis.

And once level five arrived; acceptance, London found that she wasn't ready to accept what she learned. If she could label level five of the five steps of grief it would be to burn it all down.

If Kieran wanted her to hate him more than she had before, then mission accomplished. Copper eyes looked everywhere and nowhere at the same time as London sat in the passenger seat of Kieran's car. The words still played on repeat in her head even after she tried processing everything.

Your father is my mentor.

A small chuckle escaped London's mouth as she realized her mentor was teaching her things that her father had to train him on. So in essence she was being taught by her father too.

It was official, the universe was fucking with her.

"London—"

"I'm okay. It's still a lot to take in. My father is just living life in Cerbi. Not a care in the world," London laughed to stop tears from cascading down her face.

"I know this is a lot to put on you."

"It's fine, at least I know he's safe, right?" she rationalized out loud.

"I suppose," was the only answer she received and at this point, London would gladly take it, the fewer words Kieran said, the better.

"I don't know if Jaxon told you, but he's having a pre-Adarai party before the club opens tonight to celebrate my birthday since it's actually on Adarai next week."

"That's a perfect segue to what I wanted to talk to you about actually," Kieran responded.

London hated those words already. She was sure there was nothing good that followed. She didn't respond immediately, opting to wait and hear him out.

"With the new knowledge of your true lineage, I believe it's a better idea to have you move in today instead of next week."

"That wasn't the plan." The words exploded from London's mouth with more force than she expected causing the car to shut off completely.

"I guess this will be another lesson in emotions. Turn the car back on London."

"I don't even know how I turned the car off, Kieran," she shot back.

"Use the same principle as Sight. Visualize what you want, grab the key in your mind, and turn the car on."

For a moment, London wanted to tell Kieran to take a long walk off a short cliff, but she decided against it when she saw his blue eyes become even darker. They held a look that said he was no longer playing games.

This was what London wanted, she just didn't want him to be the one teaching her. In an ideal world, her father would be showing her about their bloodline, not his protégé.

But London did as she was told and closed her eyes. Like before, she visualized the ignition to his car. The image of her hand on the key became clearer much quicker than it had at his home. Then with a deep breath, she turned the key within her mind and heard the tell-tale roar of the engine coming to life.

"I did it," the surprised gasp left her mouth as she turned toward Kieran, leaning forward for a hug. As if being burned by a fire she released him with a quiet apology and watched an unrecognizable expression cross his face.

"You should get home. We have a long day ahead of us it seems," he finally spoke adding on "with your party," after seeing the confusion on London's face.

"Right."

"Plus, you're moving in so you must have a lot of packing," he finished off.

When the lights flickered outside all London heard from the driver's side was, "Breathe."

London hated to admit it, but those words calmed her, now. Moments later the lights stopped flickering and she was calm enough to step from the car. She wanted to be a smart ass, but what good would that do?

"Nothing," London answered under her breath as she made her way to her car, leaving Kieran behind to torture her another day.

London's eyes slid over different levels of mascots at Renegades. It was obvious which were more advanced and television-quality versus which ones had been bought from stores with the word "party" in the store name.

"Excuse me," London murmured as she made her way toward the back for more napkins.

"London?"

That voice always seemed to make her smile, even now as she turned to ask, "Simon, is that you?"

"The one and only. Do you like it?"

Simon's costume wasn't much of a mascot. If she hadn't been preoccupied replaying the conversation from the previous night, she would have noticed him without any problems.

His caveman outfit was obviously from the store that had the name *Party* displayed for everyone to see.

"Nurse, I don't feel well. Can you take my temperature?"

London laughed at the smirk Simon sported as she held up a syringe full of blue liquid and said, "Open wide."

"Thanks for that nurse, I feel a lot better."

"Then my job here is done." London laughed as she turned to complete her mission to find the napkins she needed.

"Speaking of jobs, I know we work together, but would you ever consider going out with me?"

London was caught off guard by his question and flattered. And as much as she tried, she couldn't help but admire his physique in his costume. That was until she saw Kieran step forward wearing a steel gray shirt with the top two buttons undone and black slacks.

London hated to admit it, but he looked damn good, and that was unacceptable.

"I'd love that," London answered, her eyes still on Kieran as his gaze left hers and shifted to Simon.

"Awesome."

"I'm off tonight, wanna get out of here?"

"Seriously? Of course. Lead the way, nurse."

London spared Kieran one last glance as she grasped Simon's hand and allowed him to lead her out of the club.

She'd think about the consequences later, but when Simon decided his ideal date spot was Beam Me Up Java Co., London knew she made a big mistake.

Before London's thoughts could dwell on a memory of Kieran her eyes moved toward Simon and she couldn't help but smile. He was nothing like Kieran. That in itself was a great selling point for London. His emerald eyes were a stark contrast to Kieran's cobalt ones.

This man was out of her league, and he asked her out when there were hundreds of other women he could choose.

"So…Mr. Caveman, do you come here often?"

"You can call me Simon. Only my parents call me Mr. Caveman."

"Of course." London laughed, relieved that he also seemed to have a great sense of humor.

"No. This was the only quiet place I could think of that wasn't a library," Simon laughed before he turned to her and pointed toward the counter, "besides, they have coffee and Danishes."

"That they do."

"What about you? Do you come here often?" he countered.

Only with Kieran.

"No. Not really."

"To be honest, I love both coffee and Danishes, plus it gave me an excuse to feed you and hopefully make you laugh. I count that as a win."

London blushed at the mention of Simon wanting to see her outside of work. No one was interested in her recently.

His laughter was infectious. London didn't want to laugh, she wanted to wallow in her grief. Part of her thought this date would be a bust. But she was having a good time.

"This has been a great date so far. You're very sweet."

"Thank you. You're pretty sweet yourself."

It was then London noticed movement out of the corner of her eyes. "Do you need anything else?"

She hadn't seen the staff member approach her table. The Vulcan carried a tablet with her and spoke in even stilted tones. "No thank you, I'm good. How about you London?"

"All good." She smiled up at the waitress, the name *Mya* printed on her name tag.

"Very good. Live long and prosper," she said confidently with the wave of her hand.

"May the force be with you, right?"

There was a brief silence before London answered, "I don't think that's right."

"What do you mean."

"Jaxon has been schooling me in all things nerd. His words, not mine. And I think the force is Star Wars and the sign here says Star Trek."

"Oh. To be honest, I don't know the difference," Simon finally answered after pondering what London had told him. "I just figured it was like that other café across the street."

"You mean Dark Side Grind, the Star Wars café?"

"Is that not the same?"

"Simon, Simon, Simon."

"What?"

It was then London realized he was pulling her leg, "Nothing," she laughed.

At that moment, London saw Simon for the goofball he was, and it was cute. But the infatuation she thought she would feel wasn't there. She wanted it to be there, but all she felt for him was friendship. Deep down she was thinking of Kieran. She wanted to hate him more than the air she breathed.

She thought back to how she was supposed to be with him. London hoped he would have forgotten about their agreement, but she also knew that wasn't likely.

"I just remembered that I have to meet my mom for my birthday dinner."

"Isn't it next week, though."

"Yeah. Family tradition, though," London lied.

"One more hour?"

"I'm sorry, I have to leave, now."

The words left her mouth with more panic than she intended causing the café lights to flicker for a brief second.

"I'm so sorry."

"For what?!" Simon called after London as she bolted toward the door.

She just prayed that Kieran wouldn't count this against her.

FOURTEEN

Kieran whispered into his phone, his eyes moving back and forward between Mason and his computer. Mason hadn't said anything. He wasn't stupid enough to think he wouldn't rub this in his face the moment he hung up. The two had a love-hate relationship where Mason loved to make fun of Kieran for being a momma's boy and Kieran hated him for it.

"Because I'm a grown man."

Kieran watched as Mason tried to stifle a chuckle but failed. From his end of the phone it sounded like a grown man arguing with his mother. The truth was far more sinister because it was a Collector being insubordinate with his boss.

Eve wanted a progress report on the mission. The only problem was that Kieran was helping the enemy harness her abilities. This had to be what he was sent to Terra for, but it didn't explain the Shift.

The statement of being a grown man was just for show. He needed something to make the call more believable to Mason.

The man lived to be a pain in his ass, and Kieran didn't need his shit at the moment.

"She didn't seem to complain about me using her."

Kieran watched as Mason's eyebrows went up at the sound of yelling from the other end of the phone. Kieran was sure that Mason had never heard Eve yell before. She was always quiet and reserved, some even said calculating.

"Sorry, Ma'am," Kieran whispered before he removed the phone from his ear. Did she just hang up on him?

His smirk quickly faded. He must have looked like a young boy being scolded by his mother, which was exactly what Mason thought was happening. In the end it all worked out perfectly with the well-crafted lie that started once they set foot in New Haven.

"You good boss?" came a low chuckle.

"Can it, Mason!"

"Hey, don't take your anger out on me." Mason laughed standing up to his full six foot four inches. Of course, this only served to have Kieran do the same. He wasn't going to allow someone to bully him, but neither was Mason. That made Kieran trust him more. If he couldn't be bullied then he couldn't be bought, and those two things were almost synonymous.

"I'm not in the fucking mood Mason., so how about we put it away and get some work done."

"Whatever you say…Boss," Mason smiled as he turned and walked out of Kieran's home office.

The click of the door allowed Kieran to relax finally. The icy bite that wafted in from outside and clung to the room as he looked for a coat. He hadn't expected this for Terra in September. Add to the fact that it was one day closer to London's birthday, and it was the perfect weather for his mood.

She was around for almost a month at this rate, but who was counting?

The Devereux deal loomed over Kieran's head. He was too focused on London. Kieran couldn't afford to let this deal slip through his fingers.

What better way to show he was still in charge than to take something from someone else? Either way, Kieran didn't want to go into the deal off his game.

Kieran wasn't naive enough to think he could waltz in and takeover After Dark. He knew Georgia Rae Devereux wouldn't go down without a fight. All the stories claimed she was as cutthroat as any of his male counterparts. Some even described her as a lone wolf, pointing out the fact that she ran the company alone since the death of her late husband.

Her drive and strategic thinking had catapulted the company to new heights, just not high enough since they needed his cash to bail them out.

As he slipped on his shoes, Kieran looked around his barren office. Each impersonal touch was a reminder that this was not a place to call home, this was a space to sleep or fuck. It was not a place to become comfortable. The thought depressed him to the point he longed for Cerbi.

"I'll just have to make this faster than I expected." Darkness bubbled under the surface of his groomed appearance waiting to burst out. It was finally time that it got a proper hello.

Once the duo arrived at their destination they were once again in awe of the building. After Dark towered above every other structure within the city block. It was a stone structure that blanketed its neighbors, denying it a taste of sunlight. The perfect metaphor for what was to come.

Kieran never went inside but, he hoped to rain his own taste of darkness on the company once he was finished. A Devereux could never be trusted if he believed the stories handed down from generation to generation.

Kieran stood at the bottom of concrete stairs, observing the flow of traffic coming and going from the building. What he noticed was that there was an obvious hierarchy in place, he saw it time and time again, but never in one place at the same time.

Kieran stood at the bottom of the concrete stairs. From the outside there wasn't much to look at. It didn't resemble a bar, but the words After Dark were displayed in bold letters. The flow of traffic coming and going confused Kieran. It reminded him more of Chaos than anything he saw while in Terra.

It was obvious there was a hierarchy in place. Kieran saw it before but never in one place at the same time. There were suits, blazers, and coveralls.

Suits moved quickly in either direction. They were too busy to give a second thought to those around them, after all time is money. Suits wore garments that most only dreamed of and jewelry to match. And then there were blazers.

Blazers were a mix of men and women who appeared to strive being just like suits. Most looked frazzled, like they were on the edge of a nervous breakdown. Keeping up with the Joneses would do that. Only one group had the higher ground and everyone knew it was the suits.

Then there were coveralls sprinkled in amongst the two like a dark horse. Their greased appearance a sore thumb at the base of a sophisticated giant. Both suits and blazers turned their noses up at them, yet they didn't turn coveralls away.

It appeared that all were welcome under the tutelage of Georgia Rae Devereux.

"Boss?"

"You don't have to call me that Mason."

"You call me Doc." The mammoth of a man beside him smiled, both men a whopping six foot four inches. The only difference between them the shade of skin that lay hidden beneath expensive suits. The two moved in sync, a team effort that took years to perfect. Mason. knew almost everything about Kieran, even the parts of him that he tried to hide. A damaged soul knew a kindred spirit when it saw one.

"Doc isn't your name just like Boss isn't mine."

"Titles are important too, right? But remember you just said that later."

The two stepped inside a room that reminded them of a federal building, the entrance equipped with metal detectors and armed guards. "I thought this was bar deal."

"It is."

"Then why all the muscle?"

"I guess we will see," Kieran stated moving toward one of the metal detectors praying he didn't set anything off. Green lights all the way, just as he had expected. It was Mason he was worried about, a card-carrying gun owner with a license to conceal.

"Before I go through here, I do want to let you know that I have a weapon on my person, it's registered. See him, that's my boss, he's headed in for a meeting."

The two guards exchanged a brief look, "Sorry sir, we can't let any weapons in the building, registered or not."

"I see. And they can?" Mason motioned toward the two-armed guards who stood near the elevator.

"Unfortunately, you will have to remove it from the premises before we can let you enter."

Mason's eyes moved to Kieran. The two didn't need to speak, everything that needed to be said could be conveyed with a simple nod. Kieran didn't think he would need Mason for this meeting, and he knew his friend wasn't going to leave his weapon unattended.

"Give me an hour, no more, got it?"

"Yes, Boss."

"And stop calling me that!" Kieran yelled back as he watched his friend nod and then turn around, the slightest hint of a smirk on his face. *Damn old man,* he thought. Given that Mason was at least four or five years his senior, he didn't look the thirty something he was. Kieran really needed to ask him how old he was.

Once his bodyguard left the building, Kieran turned and walked toward the elevator. The meeting was on the second floor.

He never went into any deal with lies or deception, whether he was in the boardroom or the bedroom. Every party involved knew what he brought to the table.

"Let's do this," he murmured with a quick tug at his tie. Kieran just hoped the risk he was taking would be worth the reward.

For a moment Kieran didn't move, his eyes fixed on Georgia Rae's chestnut ones, unable to focus on the meeting taking place. The words from Eve becoming clearer with each passing second.

"If you see anything suspicious report back to me."

It was supposed to focus on his mission. The only problem with Kieran's logic was his mission was London. Time always seemed to slow down when Kieran thought of her. It led him to do stupid things to erase her from his mind like sleep with the vegan stripper.

Kieran hadn't touched anyone since. He hadn't wanted to.

"Don't you agree."

"I apologize. Could you repeat that again?"

The intensity he felt for London was still present. The knowledge of who she really was colliding with Eve's words. She was the daughter of a man he looked up to.

"Mr. Alexander, I thanked you for your proposal but will have to unfortunately decline."

"That was what I thought you said. You don't need help keeping yourself afloat, then?"

"I only required a new venture. Renegades doesn't fit the After Dark aesthetic."

"How so?"

"No offense Mr. Alexander, but Renegades clientele dress and behave as if they are frequenting a brothel."

"No offense, huh?"

"I only mean that my patrons might find it difficult aligning my core beliefs with your establishment. For that reason, I must decline your offer."

Kieran could sense a hint of fear in her voice and decided not to drop the subject.

"It seems we are at an impasse Ms. Devereux.

"Yes, it seems like it, and you can call me Georgia Rae."

"Of course, Georgia Rae," Kieran chuckled back, his eyes holding her gaze. Georgia Rae's smile faded momentarily; her eyes shifted to the left for a moment.

She's lying.

"It's better this way." Kieran stood from his seat, his hand moving to button his jacket.

"What do you mean?"

"When this place goes bankrupt, and it will, we'll be able to purchase it for pennies on the dollar. It'll be a win for us."

Silence filled the space until Georgia Rae finally spoke up. "Wait! Surely, we can talk about this again. Give me a month to think about it. This is a big decision."

"I'll give you till Adarai."

"That's in less than two weeks!" Georgia Rae exclaimed

"And because I'm so generous I'll have a check written out to you ready. Unless you think After Dark can hold on longer."

When she didn't say anything, Kieran couldn't help but admire her. She was a worthy adversary. It was a shame what was hers would be his and Devereux would be a name whispered and lost among the wind.

FIFTEEN

The knock-on London's door startled her and then made her smile. After she left the café, Simon had made a point to message her every day. He even joked about knowing where she lived and would be happy to say hi to her mom. London had declined, but it looked like he didn't listen.

"Simon, I said not to come over," she responded, opening the door without looking through her peephole. She was dressed in her silk robe but didn't mind Simon getting a little eye candy before she sent him on his way.

"Simon?"

Standing before her was not Simon Monroe. How she wished it was, but instead the only thing that came out of her mouth was, "Kieran?"

Each name spoken over the other was masked with confusion and eventually anger. How dare he come to her home without giving her a heads up.

"What are you doing here, Kieran?"

"Is this where you went when you left Renegades?"

"That's none of your business." London's chin lifted slightly; her anger palpable as she watched the judgment spread on his face.

She was a grown woman and could keep company with any red-blooded man she saw fit. Hand placed at the curve of her waist, just above her hip, London looked up at Kieran waiting for a reply from him. When Kieran did not respond, London's eyes rolled back into her head, and a loud sigh escaped.

"If you're not going to tell me why you're here, you need to leave. I have plans."

"With Simon?"

The question was cocked and ready to explode no matter what response London provided. Her eyes moved down to his chest, the half-buttoned shirt putting his smooth chest on display. The muscles moved beneath it in tandem with his breathing as he waited for a reply. He was mad, and London loved it.

"My relationship with Simon is none of your business."

London took a step back, hand poised on the door. Silence lingered between the two for too long. London refused to allow Kieran to drag her into whatever game he was playing. She didn't enjoy having her feelings toyed with, and Simon showed her good guys did exist.

"You need to leave."

Finally, someone with half a brain had spoken, and it was her. The door swung toward Kieran only to stop before it closed completely. Large hands moved the door back into its original position with too much force. Copper eyes moved back to her tormentor's face to see his cobalt eyes had darkened.

The storm that brewed behind them matched every look he gave her since she met him. The only difference now was London refused to let his baby blues manipulate her.

"Kieran, I'm about to pack. I will meet you at your place in a couple of hours."

"I think I'll wait."

"What?"

"I don't mind waiting."

London was taken back by Kieran's response. She watched him walk into her kitchen out of spite. She knew from her experience so far, he could be cruel, but she didn't know he could be intrusive as well.

"Kieran, I will pack my shit and meet you at your place in a couple of hours."

"I'll stay and make sure you pack everything you need. You're gonna be there for a while. I wouldn't want you to forget something."

London moved toward her kitchen determined to get him out of her home before her mother got back. She had gone to her book club, and it wouldn't be ideal to have a Collector standing in her kitchen.

Even now, as she watched him lean against her kitchen counter she couldn't help but want to throttle him and kiss him.

He needed to go.

"You know what, I'll call Simon, maybe he can help me too."

London knew it was a mistake once the words slipped through her lips. It was an even bigger mistake the second she turned her back to him, but it was too late to erase her error.

It was apparent when her back fell into his body, her ass pressed against what she could only imagine was his hard-on. "You know, I like it when you're being a Sam."

"I don't know what that is, and you know it."

"Depends on how you look at it. Some say it stands for smart ass mouth, but the circle I run in prefer smart ass masochist."

"Masochist?"

As much as London told herself she needed to move away from him, deep down inside, her body craved his lips pressed against hers again.

"Both are fitting really." Kieran ignored London's indignation at the use of the word masochist.

"Masochist?" London repeated louder making sure Kieran addressed her question.

"Forgive me. A masochist is—"

"I know what a masochist is Kieran!"

She was no masochist.

"Why would you call me that?"

"It would appear you like a little pain with your pleasure Ms. Reign."

"That's not true—"

Before London could finish her sentence, Kieran's turned her toward him, his lips crashing against hers.

The kiss began soft and quickly turned into something much more impatient. She couldn't help but wrap her arms around Kieran's neck as he turned her body until it met the counter behind him.

The hardness of the marble slab pressed against her back, but what London focused on was Kieran's body pressed tightly against hers.

London's body involuntarily arched toward him, urging him to continue. A positive sign in the right direction because Kieran grabbed London's ass with both hands and hoisted her up his body. With a small yelp, London wrapped her legs around his waist, feeling the cold countertop below her bare thighs.

Kieran's hands eased down her body gently as they slid up the inside of her thighs, parting them slowly. Heat spread across her face as she watched a smirk emerge. He was enjoying this.

"Lift your ass."

London hated herself for listening to him, but she did as he asked and used her core to hover over the counter. She watched with hooded lids as Kieran pulled her underwear down her thighs and past her knees. His hand massaged her foot briefly before liberating her panties from her ankles and then quickly placing the flimsy material into his jacket pocket.

"Hey! Those are mine."

"Not anymore."

"But—"

"How about we play a game. We'll call it Kieran says."

"Really?" London asked knowing what he was doing by changing the name.

"Let's start now. Kieran says don't speak."

"Kieran—ow!"

"Oh, did I forget to tell you that the consequence for breaking the rules was a light tap to the thighs?"

"No! You did not!"

"Oops," was all Kieran said as he smirked and rubbed his calloused hands over the stinging flesh.

"You call that a light tap?!" London tried to ignore the stinging she felt radiating from her skin.

"Let's try this again. Kieran says don't speak."

London instantly opened her mouth and then promptly closed it when she saw Kieran's hand lift from its resting place beside her legs.

"Very good, Sam."

London knew it was a trick. She hated the name even more, especially since she knew the true meaning.

"My name is London."

London braced herself for the stinging pain of his palm meeting her other thigh. Instead, she felt his hand cover where her underwear had once been. The other hand slowly made its way up her stomach, its slow climb over her closed robe excruciating.

"No bra?"

Without waiting for an answer, Kieran's nimble fingers brushed over the exposed nipples, rolling each between his thumb and index finger.

Warmth replaced the twinge of pain and pleasure spread through her body as Kieran placed one rosebud into his mouth to suckle before pulling on it carefully. London's voice cracked with pleasure. She wanted to tell him to stop, but more than anything, she wanted him to finish what he started.

London felt Kieran's teeth nip the exposed skin only to pull on the other exposed nipple. Her entire body felt like it was on fire. When Kieran's response was to moan, London knew she was in trouble. She felt the moisture between her thighs slowly pool on the counter beneath her body and for the first time in a long time, she craved another person's touch beside her own.

Her eyes caught Kieran's crooked smirk as his hand contacted with her wet center with a forceful smack.

"Fuck!"

London's eyes opened as pain and pleasure moved through her body as she orgasmed. The smirk on his face told London he thought he won. At this moment he had. But before this got further out of hand, she needed to stop everything.

"We need to stop before we both regret this."

"Kieran says lay back."

"Kier—," London's mouth shut when she felt his hand raise again.

"Now you're getting it," he whispered, "But if at any time you want me to stop, say blueberry, and I'll go. Do you understand?"

London nodded her head, but that didn't satisfy Kieran's insatiable need to make her submit.

"Kieran says you can answer me verbally. Do you understand?"

"Yes."

Smack.

"Yes?"

"Yes, Sir?"

"Very good. Now do what Kieran says."

For a brief moment, London almost jumped down and ran. She didn't know why she was even allowing him to speak to her in such a manner. But deep down she liked it, and that made her even more confused.

As she complied London felt large hands slide between her thighs to stroke her pussy. London cried out, her back arching toward his touch, as her hips bucked toward Kieran's hand.

Her eyes opened wide once Kieran's mouth covered hers with a kiss. When her body began to relax, London felt Kieran push two fingers into her dripping core. His fingers moved rapidly in and out of her.

London's body begin to tremble prompting Kieran to quicken his pace. London couldn't help the orgasm that ripped through her body as she stiffened and screamed her release.

"Kieran!"

Her body slowly drifted back down as she opened her eyes.

Kieran looked at her, a new primal look of desire there. She couldn't help but smile at him as he leaned forward to kiss her on the forehead.

"Reign," he whispered beside her ear.

"Yes."

"Tell Simon he's got competition."

"Blueberry," London whispered, the mood officially broken. She was an idiot for allowing anything to happen.

With the nod of his head, Kieran kissed her one last time and walked toward her door to leave, but not before saying, "You have two hours."

God, she hated him.

SIXTEEN

The door creaked open like an omen as Mason peeked his head in and finally his whole body. Kieran turned around from his office window looking out at downtown New Haven, his body tense from his thoughts.

After a few minutes of standing in silence, Kieran watched Mason open his mouth and then quickly close it. "Boss."

"You know, I always used to wish I owned a place like this. Only it would be some place that looked over the city. When my family moved to New Haven, I hated it. Hated it because it was such a small town and I'd never get my wish. Do you know what I wish for now?"

"To not be so dramatic."

"Silence."

Silence followed this revelation before Kieran began to speak again. "Now I have you antagonizing me for no reason and London making me question everything.

"Speaking of London, she's—"

"Here," Kieran finished. "Yeah, I know, I saw her today."

"You did?"

"Yes, Mason. I did."

"You're taking it a lot better than I thought you would."

Kieran moved towards his desk for the first time since Mason came into his office. "Taking what better?"

"All the flirting between Simon and London."

The fuck they were!

"With it being on company time, of course," Mason finished.

Silence lingered once more as Kieran's hands clenched into fists. He should be working on his proposal to Georgia Rae Devereux. He had enough on his mind. He didn't have time to add Simon and London's exploits too.

"I'm sure it's nothing."

"I thought the same thing until I saw them get into a car and leave together," Mason added sitting down in the chair across from Kieran.

"What!?" Kieran cleared his throat and adjusted his tie before he lowered his voice and repeated, "What?"

"Yeah. About thirty minutes ago. So . . . you didn't know?"

"Mason—"

"I know. I'll leave. Maybe I'll head to the Garden and see what the girls are doing."

"Good idea."

Kieran's eye twitched as he thought of the two of them alone in a car. His gaze moved towards the clock on his desk, it was lunch time. Logic warranted they went gone to lunch, but even that was too much time together. Simon was playing the long game and Kieran was trying not to fall behind.

His thoughts drifted back to the night before. He could still hear the sound of her moans spilling over her lips. She was extremely vocal. Kieran liked that about her. He only went over to discuss training, but the sound of Simon's name from her lips set him off.

"It's just lunch. That's it. Lunch."

Kieran repeated the words "just lunch" a few more times before he heard a knock to his office door. He didn't have time for anymore of Mason's shit. It took him less steps than usual to reach his door, pulling it open with a boisterous, "What?!"

"Shit!"

There at his door stood London, holding her chest. Her bosom heaved up and down with the sound of her labored breaths. Kieran could get used to this sight.

"Sorry."

London's breathing came out in spurts as she stepped in and held an aluminum foil wrapped object out towards Kieran.

"What's this?"

He watched as London's eyes rolled. She never dropped her hand, instead, she moved it up and down a little before saying, "A taco. Want it?"

"You got me food?"

"I got me food and overestimated my hunger. Do you want the taco or not?"

It was clear that she was becoming angry. Good. He would work with this. If she could keep her anger at bay, then it was proof their sessions were taking root.

"I want lots of things."

Kieran's eyes drifted from London's face back to her chest. Her breathing was under control now. "I am hungry, but I think you have something else that I'd much rather taste."

"Mr. Alexander, I don't think that would be appropriate. It should never have happened to begin with."

"I think we are far beyond things being appropriate with us Ms. Reign."

Two could play that game.

"Well, all I have to offer you is this taco. Take it or leave it."

"Is that what the younger generation is calling pussy now, I'd much rather have that."

"Well, people in hell want ice water, but they can't get that shit either. God! I'm not having sex with you."

"Okay. You aren't having sex with me," Kieran repeated London's words with a smirk planted on his face.

"You're an asshole." The taco hit his chest before it fell to the ground, "Eat it. Don't eat it. I don't fucking care."

"You curse a lot." Kieran's hand moved to catch her wrist before she left. London's eyes moved to where his flesh met hers, but he didn't remove his hand.

"I hadn't noticed."

"I can make sure you stop. Wanna know how?"

Please ask how.

"Not really."

"You sure?"

"Positive."

Kieran pulled London against his body with a yelp. "I think you'd like it."

"And what is that?"

"Being bent over my desk, getting your ass spanked. I think you'd love that shit," Kieran mocked London. "Want to test out my theory?"

Kieran was sure he piqued London's interest. His hand making the journey toward her ass until he heard voices moving toward them.

"Another time, Sam."

"That's not my name."

"Isn't it?"

Kieran watched London turn and disappear from his office. He needed to pull back on his possessiveness. She wasn't his to possess. But that didn't stop him from wanting to try.

London walked from the back of Renegades with her hand over her heart. She was finding it harder to be cavalier to Kieran. Sure, she hadn't gotten laid in a while, but she needed to pull herself together. It was a little foreplay, that was all. She didn't need or want to fawn all over him. She had better things to do with her time, like go out with Simon again.

He suggested bowling and London immediately said yes. He was the type of guy she should be spending her time with. Not Kieran.

"Lonny, there you are!"

London's heart quickened once more at the sound of Simon's voice. How could she be attracted to both men?

I'm not attracted to Kieran.

London knew a lie when she thought one. And that was a bold-faced lie. Even if her mind hated him, her body was all in. She couldn't even offer him food without the possibility there might be some form of inappropriate touching. And he was part owner so who was going to stop him.

Not me.

"Damn it, London."

"What was that Lonny?"

She meant to whisper but of course in true London fashion everything she wanted was going to hell.

"Oh. Nothing. Just forgot my food in the back."

"Why were you in the back?"

Yes. Why was she in the back?

"There was a problem with clocking in and I wanted to talk to Jaxon about it."

"He's not here," Simon offered the insight London already knew. She was happy to see he didn't question she might be lying. Instead, he believed her, no questions asked. She was an awful person.

"Yeah. I know that now," she offered with the fakest laugh she could muster.

"Know what?"

"Jesus!"

Did she accidentally summon him?

"Did I scare you?"

"No. I just scream Jesus for no reason."

"I can give you a reason," Kieran's voice echoed in London's head.

The words were pushed into her head with no effort. His voice like silk, filled her head erasing any other background thoughts or noise. It kind of tickled, but more than anything it caused her to panic. If he could invade her head, did that mean he could hear her thoughts as well?

How the hell had he done that?

"Practice," was all he said aloud.

That answered her question.

"Huh?" London heard Simon say. She had forgotten Simon was standing with her. Great, he probably thinks she is crazy or worse, Kieran and her had some kind of weird thing going on. They did, but she didn't want Simon to know.

"Don't worry about it," Kieran answered before she could. "Speaking of practice, I'll need you to stay late tomorrow."

"Why?"

"Because I'm your boss and I requested you stay late tomorrow."

London knew that the word boss held a double meaning in this moment. He held what he knew over her head like a pendulum. She waited each day for it to swing a little closer to her, threatening to cut her in half.

Well, not today.

"No can do."

"What do you mean, you can't?"

"I mean, I can't. Simon and I have a date."

"Really?" The two men spoke simultaneously.

"Yes. Really," London paused before saying, "Tomorrow at eight, we're going to mini golf."

London could see the muscles in Kieran's face tense as his jaw clenched. Good. He deserved a little bit of misery for all the shit he was putting her through.

"Sorry, Mr. Alexander."

That was the final straw, London could see it written on his face as Kieran nodded his head and turned to walk away.

London knew she was kicking the hornet's nest, but she'd be damned if she let Kieran Alexander get his way.

SEVENTEEN

Georgia Rae knew she was royally screwed. Not only did she not have the money to put into After Dark, but she also didn't have the money to pay Wes. She hoped he was dumber than he seemed on the phone and didn't check all of the money at the meeting.

She just needed to get in and get out as fast as she could. He refused to push up the date but now she needed him to more than ever. Wes didn't realize the gold he was sitting on. When she thought of London Reign all she saw were dollar signs. All Georgia Rae needed was a vial of her blood and she was golden.

Georgia Rae just needed a way to spin the narrative to fit her own agenda. After all, she was a member of the Tribunal, and her betrayal could land her in a cell in Styxx. The idea barely on the tip of her tongue as she thought back to the conversation with Wes.

The phone rang mercilessly, each short twill drowning out her thoughts. The Maxwell E. Devereux Hall of the New Haven country club housed several colleagues of Georgia Rae. Each one owed her a favor, and it was time her debts all came due.

The hall named after her late husband held the only Conduit known to access the Citadel. Only those recruited into the Tribunal knew of its existence. Every ten years an election was held and new member was appointed a seat among the council. Nepotism ran deep within each house. The only way to vote out a member was to challenge them. And no one within Chaos was brave enough to ruin centuries of tradition. Seats in the Tribunal were passed down generation to generation.

It paid to be rich in a time where money talked above everything else. It didn't hurt to be covered in privilege as well, and Georgia Rae was spoiled rotten. Several people wandered the halls of the country club, each individual keeping her away from the room she desperately needed to enter. When she saw her opening, Georgia Rae placed her hand against the mirror next to a door labeled Faculty Lounge.

"Out of the darkness we bring light."

"One goal," an automated voice spoke.

"One destiny," Georgia Rae smiled as she stepped forward through the Conduit. The mirror returned to its rightful place as it closed behind her.

Georgia Rae thought it was clever to hide the automated system within what looked like a thermostat. No one was the wiser, and the organization stayed under the radar.

The Citadel was nestled safely behind the only entrance beneath the city of New Haven. It was lovingly named that due to its cathedral ceiling.

No one truly knew how it all worked, one moment Georgia Rae was in one time, one space, and now she wasn't. Many speculated that it was Chaos Magic passed down from generation to generation. Others speculated it was from a time too dark to remember and too dangerous to bear repeating.

As one of the many members of the Tribunal, Georgia Rae knew what London Reign's Resurrection meant to all those who lived and breathed the Vlosyrós Law.

There was but one goal...one destiny, and Georgia Rae was championed to make that destiny a reality. If that meant killing the only person who could help her, then so be it. Sacrifices had to be made for the greater good.

"I take it you being here is not good." The calm feminine voice caught Georgia Rae off guard. The soft click of heels muted by carpeted floors.

"Why do you say that?"

"You vowed to not step foot in here again until the mission was complete, and from what I've heard you have a long way to go."

"I wouldn't say a long way. The end is in sight," Georgia Rae smiled, although it did not reach her eyes.

"Is that so?"

"It is."

"And how is that going," the calm feminine voice asked.

The statuesque and voluptuous figure screamed power. Everyone in the Tribunal knew her to be by the book, which worked for the head of Collectors. Voluminous honey blonde curls framed her face and pulled attention to the eye makeup around her brown eyes. Not much information was available about her, but the one thing everyone knew was not to fuck with Khaiv Rexton.

"Khaiv, I didn't realize you'd be here this evening."

"I can say the same thing to you Georgia Rae and call me Eve."

"My apologies," Georgia Rae smiled with a nod.

I have one of my people looking into the breach. But I'd love to hear your plan on bringing in the Eldite."

"I have located her."

"Already?"

"I have my sources. There's a fox circling her as we speak. All I need now is to let it lead her to me."

"And this fox...are they a reliable source?"

"The best."

"They better be."

Eve smiled at Georgia Rae before she turned to make her rounds with the other members. The council member for Cerbi, and all the Collectors, moved through the room with grace, the unspoken threat ramping up Georgia Rae's anxiety.

And with Wes in the wind and not answering her calls, Georgia Rae was secretly starting to panic.

"Damn freelancers."

Georgia Rae would have to do all the hard work herself she mused. She always hated getting her hands dirty, but sometimes she had to get down and dirty like the best of them. After all, it was one goal…one destiny.

Georgia Rae stepped through the Conduit returning to the country club in Terra, her mind still reeling from seeing Eve in New Haven, standing before her.

Wes needed to answer his phone if she was going to explain to him the new changes. While it was short notice, it was important to know what was set in motion.

When the phone instantly went to voicemail, Georgia Rae knew she needed to do something fast or all hell was going to break loose. While Wes was revered in the circles that knew him, only Eve knew of his existence.

Georgia Rae was determined to show them all that she could delegate and execute a plan just like everyone else, even better if she pulled her coup off. Her only missing link was Wes.

"Where are you?"

Georgia Rae looked at her phone, the anger bubbling under the surface as she pressed send once more and listened to the voicemail's automated voice tell her to leave a message. This didn't bode well for her or the Tribunal. She knew there would be hell to pay if anything else fell apart.

Wes watched as the day slowly morphed into night. The stage was being set for a concert in the center of town. It was the perfect cover for what he needed to do in the coming days. First Street was littered with inebriated bodies celebrating a week-long celebration leading up to the big night, unaware of the danger they were all in.

Idiots. All of them.

Wes didn't need a large crowd to blend in. He used his smile and charismatic charm to lure most people to him, both men and women. He didn't care much for men, but in a pinch, he wouldn't object to seducing one if the ends justified the means.

His lean muscular frame and chiseled features could place him in any magazine. His good looks were the first thing that caught the attention of his prizes. It helped that he had just the right amount of influence to suggest that they both go to a second location.

His prizes never hesitated to leave with him. Why would they when they never looked deeper? On the surface, he was harmless. By the time they finally saw past the good looks it was too late. They realized Wes was a stone-cold killer.

"Excuse you!"

The voice slurred as cold liquid moved down the sleeve of Wes' sweater. Alcohol lingered in the air as he looked down at the man standing before him, he was a few inches shorter but had enough liquid courage to make the mistake of coming at Wes.

"Excuse you!" the drunk yelled not waiting for an answer. His body language screamed he wanted a fight, and the itch that Wes felt beneath the surface began to claw to be released.

He wouldn't kill him, not in public, but it might give him something else to fixate on to hold him over until he met his next mark.

"Hey man, Lori's looking for you, come on."

"Lucky," the drunk man slurred as he turned and stumbled toward his friends. *Lucky indeed*, Wes thought as he veered to the left and moved away from the crowd.

Music blared through the night air, polluting the area with audible sex and death.

Fake Dominique was a means to an end, there could only be one and after seeing his new prize Wes could finally see that this woman who proclaimed her name was Shannon wasn't who he thought she was.

Once again his phone rang, the number blocked, but Wes knew who it was, Georgia Rae. With the click of a button he sent her to voicemail, he would talk to her once the next stage of his plan was complete.

"Hey baby, wanna party?" Wes's eyes landed on a woman dressed as a scantily clad cat, a slutty cat some would say. Her skin complexion was all wrong, pale even under the full moon, but the itch was strong, and Wes would have to make a small sacrifice tonight.

"Of course." He smiled his million-dollar smile. "I have just the thing in mind."

"I'm Candace, but all my friends call me Candy," she beamed, her blonde hair pulled up in a high ponytail. The makeup caked her face, a sign that she took pride in her appearance and she'd be just another pretty face posted on fliers.

"Classy name, for a classy woman," Wes mused, already coming up with the things he wanted to do to her.

"Thanks! My mom hates when I call myself Candy, she doesn't find it classy, as you put it. She thinks it sounds cheap, but I love it. I feel sexy just hearing other people say it. Did you know—"

The first thing Wes would have to do is sew her mouth shut, her incipit voice was getting on his nerves. Her words were not important enough to continue listening to. They wouldn't matter until he said they did. Right now was a necessary evil, if Wes wanted her to come with him. He needed her trust.

Besides shallow women trusted a man who fed into their vanity.

"And all he thought about was some stupid girl named London, can you believe that."

"Wait, go back for a second. Who only thought of a stupid girl?"

"This guy I was seeing," she continued, "I asked around after he pretty much dumped me."

"That's awful," Wes ramped up the sympathy, his plans changing drastically.

"She's not even his type and he's still pining away for her, how pathetic is that? You know what I mean?"

Wes didn't know what she meant but smiled and nodded all the same. He could tell she believed she was winning him over. Candy might be just the person to get him closer to London without Georgia Rae being the wiser.

"I have a proposition for you if you're willing and able," Wes whispered putting on his best fake smile.

"Oooo…what kind of proposition?"

"One that will get you the man you want, the guy who's obsessed with the stupid girl, what was her name…London?"

Candy paused before she nodded her head. "Deal."

"Great. I'm Wes, by the way. But all my friends call me Simon."

EIGHTEEN

Heavy panting filled the air, its melodic sound keeping beat to the pounding in Kieran's chest. Adrenaline pumped through his veins, overflowing with malice as another one carelessly zoomed by.

What would it take to stop them?

Rope?

Tape?

Death?

No, death was too harsh.

Kieran winced as another ran by, splashing water from a puddle nearby. Laughter drifted toward him as more ran by. Children, like the Black Death only this time disguised by rosy cheeks and annoying giggling.

The laughter did not work on Kieran. He could see right through their facade and knew they were secretly plotting.

With Adarai so close it wasn't a surprise that the entire city was on candy patrol. What bothered Kieran the most was how they rushed past him with no regard for their safety or the safety of others. How he hated their small statures. They were nothing but trouble. Trouble he didn't need tonight.

Adarai was his least favorite of Terra's holidays for this reason. Not because he had to hear the words Trick or Treat repeatedly. But because what was really out there would make the bleached carcasses of the fake skeletons draped upon doorsteps look like what they were. Child's play.

Boards creaked menacingly as he shifted his weight. He watched their cult move in droves from house to house only to repeat their ritual once more.

It's not Adarai yet. Was this practice for the big day?

Kieran never could understand Undesirables fascination with the awful day. The stench of sweet confections was mixed in with the foul odor of malevolence and masked with oversexed emotion. In his opinion nothing good could come out of the day. Hopefully tonight would change his mind.

The cold bit into him as he clung to his Ralph Lauren trench coat. The onyx material flapping behind him with each gust of arctic breeze, which was unusual for this time of the year in this part of Terra.

Jack-o-lanterns cackled from a distance as the lights placed inside them flickered violently. Their warped smiles luring many to its sinister glow.

Normally around this time of the year in New Haven it would be warm enough to go outside without a jacket, but today was not one of those days. Snow cascaded down, joining the remaining of its brothers and sisters.

The wind moaned its satisfaction as children ran down the street against its icy breath. Their mascots hid underneath warm coats as more parents screamed at them to be careful.

The sun had finally set, casting a sickly gray hue on the street. The faint appearance of clouds floated toward another part of town in the distance, leaving behind a glimmer of stars.

Kieran's eyes traveled from the small menaces to the door before him.

London was given instructions and out of spite, she had ignored them. With his fist poised to knock on the door, he was caught off guard when it opened.

"Kieran? What are you doing here?"

"We had an agreement that you would train with me whenever I told you, Sam."

"Kieran—"

"And you broke that agreement," Kieran continued.

"Now is not the—"

"Who's at the door, Lonny?"

"—time," London finished quietly as Simon stepped into the room.

"Hey Stone, fancy seeing you here."

Kieran wanted to wipe that stupid smirk off Simon's face. Instead, he opted to do something he never did, be petty.

"I thought I forgot something from the other day, was just coming back to get what's mine."

"I don't think you left anything here. Maybe you should check your home." London's voice was tight, the intent obvious in her voice. She wanted him to leave.

"I'm pretty sure this isn't at my home. Went missing a few days ago, here as a matter of fact."

"You were here?" Simon cut into the conversation.

"Yeah. London even asked me to come."

Kieran knew the last part was a jab toward London, but he couldn't find a fuck to give.

"I didn't realize y'all were such close friends," Kieran's voice came out gruffer than he wanted.

"I hope to be more than that after tonight."

The intent behind the statement was not lost on Kieran as he watched Simon's smile spread across his face. The knives were out, and the dual of words had begun. Simon was issuing a warning of his own.

"Is that so?" Kieran asked London, noticing her embarrassment from being put on the spot.

"Kieran, we were just leaving."

"Where to?" He knew where they were going, he made a mental note the day London mentioned it at work.

"Mini golf at Hole in One," Simon interjected.

"Sounds great. Which one are we going to?" Kieran asked as he turned to head back toward his car.

"That wasn't an invitation. You aren't —"

"The one off of Main Street," Simon interjected.

"I'll meet you there." Kieran yelled over his shoulder as he walked toward the same screaming children he secretly wished death.

"Kieran—you're not invited."

The words echoed on a breeze and faded away. If Simon wanted a war, he'd get one.

London couldn't believe the audacity of Kieran to invite himself on her date with Simon. Even though it technically wasn't a date, he didn't know that. Now he was staking his claim on her. All it took was a little bit of danger, a lot of inappropriate touching, and now she was supposed to be his. She thought not.

Then why did the thought of him being jealous make her readjust herself in her seat? London prayed that Simon didn't notice. She planned on putting her encounter with Kieran out of her mind, and then BAM! There he was, on her doorstep.

"Did you hear me?"

"I'm sorry?"

"Kieran, he's the guy, right? The one you're hung up on? The reason I'm in the friend zone?"

"I'm not—"

"It's okay. I know he's the guy, but if he thinks his tough guy act is gonna run me away, he's got another thing coming," Simon cut in, his voice laced with determination.

One more reason for London to feel like an asshole. She had already let Kieran win, and he didn't even deserve it. Simon had done everything the right way, and she still let Kieran slip in. Not anymore.

"You aren't in the friend zone," London answered, leaning in to kiss Simon, agreeing with herself to let her encounter with Kieran be the last one.

"Wow," she heard Simon's surprised laugh before turning away from him. Just what she was afraid of. She felt nothing.

"So, how good are you at golf? I feel like you have a home court advantage since you suggested this particular miniature course."

"I've dabbled," London laughed.

"I bet."

London enjoyed his laugh. She could listen to it all day. Yeah, she could do this. She could try to get lost in Simon's emerald eyes compared to Kieran's blue ones. All she had to do was get Kieran out of her head.

Hole in One was booming. With Adarai right around the corner, a party vibe lingered.

London couldn't focus on any of that with Kieran staring at her with his fuck me eyes.

"Shit," London cursed as she hit her golf ball toward the right.

"Distracted?" Kieran smirked.

"You wish."

"There's a lot of things I wish for. That isn't it, Sam."

"Sam?"

"You don't know about Sam? I thought you would," Kieran goaded.

"No, but I need to hear this now," Simon laughed just as his phone went off. "Give me a minute to grab this, it's important."

"Of course," London smiled through clenched teeth as she watched her fake date walk off while answering his phone with the word, "Yo."

"What are you doing, Kieran?"

"What does it look like?" he countered back.

"It looks like you're being a real big dic—"

"Sorry to have to do this, but I have to go," Simon cut in.

"Already? We just got here." London was disappointed their evening would have to be cut short.

"Jaxon needs my help with preparations for Saturday."

"That sucks. Do you need any help?"

"Always."

"You want London to help you do your work," Kieran interjected into the conversation.

After a brief moment of silence, Simon said, "Of course not."

"Don't worry about him. I'll miss you," London pouted, she wanted to make sure Kieran saw how unaffected by him she was.

"Me too," Simon replied moving to London and planting a kiss on her right in front of Kieran.

"Rain check?"

"Of course. I'll talk to you later," London whispered leaning in to give Simon another small kiss.

"Call you later?"

"I'd like that." London smiled; her eyes focused solely on Simon until he walked out of the building.

"Guess it's just you and me."

London's heart skipped a beat before she turned toward Kieran. Who needed to worry about the Tribunal when she had him?

NINETEEN

The wheels on London's suitcase shouted their protest as they neared the door to Kieran's home. What guest needed their own house? There was exactly one week until Adarai, her birthday.

London was relieved when she realized she wouldn't have to live in the same space with Kieran. That would make whatever feelings she was having more tolerable. She needed distance from him more than she needed air at this point.

"Well, thanks for making sure I got here. Bye."

"You're not gonna invite me in?"

"Nope."

"What if there's someone in there? I should check just to be sure."

"Maybe he'll kill me," London murmured as the lock clicked.

"Sam—"

"No!" London's body whirled around to face him for this part of the conversation. "You are not doing that. We are not doing this." She motioned between the two of them for emphasis.

"But you know you want to," Kieran's raspy voice whispered.

"No," London said trying to hold on to her conviction.

"What's he got that I don't?"

"A genuine interest in me. Plus, he won't lead me to my death if I say no to him".

"You think I'd turn you in if you tell me no? If I wanted to let the Tribunal know of your existence, they'd already know."

"So reassuring."

"I'm doing this for both of us. I'm doing it because I like you, damn it!" Kieran yelled before he finished with, "The Tribunal has a member from each province. That's five houses that want you dead. And I don't want that."

"Of course, not," London whispered pushing into her new home still reeling from Kieran's revelation. It was obviously a lie she surmised as she quickly moved to close the door, but Kieran was too fast. He side-stepped the swinging door and moved into the living room.

"I don't have time for this. Just look around or use whatever lame excuse you have then leave."

"So feisty," Kieran smirked moving toward her.

"Nope," London moved just in time to avoid Kieran's advances. "You don't want me, Kieran. You just don't want Simon to have me."

"That's not true."

"Isn't it?"

"I want you very much and I also don't want Simon to have you."

"Whatever."

"Every time I think of him touching you I want to send him to Adon myself."

"Don't say that."

"Why?" Kieran advanced on London like a wolf stalking prey. "Don't want your boyfriend hurt?"

"You don't want me. You want to possess me."

"You're right. Let me show you," Kieran stated before his lips crashed onto hers.

The intensity took London by surprise until she forgot she was supposed to hate him. She spent all day training herself to never fall for his trap again, and here she was after her interrupted date with Simon, kissing Kieran.

Her hands were pinned above her head, her back against a wall she hadn't known was there. The hard surface prevented her from escaping.

"Don't move."

"You don't want to say Kieran says?"

"There's my Sam." Kieran smirked with the nip of his teeth against London's bottom lip. His hand tugged her shirt over her head to expose her heaving bosom.

London's black lace bra hugged her breast tightly, conforming to her body like a glove as her chest moved up and down trying to catch her breath. It took all of London's willpower to keep her hands above her head.

Kieran removed his hands the moment he realized London wouldn't try to run.

She watched as he lowered his head and kissed her exposed skin where the fabric met her body. This particular item appeared to be his favorite.

"This one looks different," he murmured into her flushed skin.

"It's a bralette," London gasped as his tongue moved against the rough material, flicking at her rosebud.

London pressed her hand softly against his head. She tried her best to be conscious of the amount of pressure she used. Sometimes she didn't know her strength and she didn't want one of those times to be now.

All logic left her as she felt him flick the bud again, this time a little harder. Not wanting to wait any longer she moved her hands away and pulled the front of her bra down to expose the chocolate buds. The cold air only made them harder.

This time when he lowered his head, Kieran slowly took her nipple into his mouth and gently suckled it. She couldn't help the gasp that escaped or the moan that followed. His attention gravitated to the other nipple seconds later to capture it in his mouth. The sensation of his tongue pushed her slightly over the edge until she was pushing his head closer to her breast, threatening to suffocate him.

Another moan escaped her mouth as Kieran moved away from the rigid surface of the wall. With her body still plastered to his, London felt what she imagined was his erection. She couldn't stop the moan that escaped her mouth. Her body bounced a second later as he placed her on the couch. There she watched as he stared at her half-naked body, his eyes devouring every inch of her.

London's hair wildly pushed against the pillows, her breast heaving rapidly from the passion she felt.

"Kieran says raise your hips."

London listened to the whispered words and rolled her eyes. The stubborn part of her wanted to tell him, no. That part of her brain hadn't gotten around to clueing her libido in. She did exactly as he asked and slowly lifted her hips.

Once she had, Kieran peeled the satin shorts down her thighs until they were at her feet, slowly kissing her calves as he did. London could feel the moisture seeping through her panties and wondered if Kieran would notice.

London felt her shorts vanish only to be replaced by Kieran's lips on the inside of her thigh. Another moan left her body, as she tangled her fingers in his hair. She only ever experienced this feeling with him. The sensations of slowly dying only he could pull from her body.

Passing her wet sex, London watched with hooded eyes as Kieran moved over his body above hers and stared into her eyes again.

London could feel his erection pressing against her completely soaked panties. Her hands clutched onto his shoulders as his lips crashed against her, the kiss rapidly becoming more demanding. London's hips moved of their own volition, trying to get as close to him as possible.

As he smiled down at her, he let his fingers trail down her smooth skin, starting at her collarbone. When he got to the waistband of her panties, he gently grasped the sides and slid them down over her hips.

London didn't need him to command her to lift her hips. She wanted to beg him to kiss the inside of her thigh again.

He eased her panties down over her feet and dropped them beside him on the floor. The look in his eyes was primal as he stared down at her body. He used his index and middle finger to playfully walk down her body. The laugh that escaped London was breathless until his fingers stopped at the top of the apex of her thighs.

He allowed the two fingers to slowly slide down between her legs where they found her clit and began to massage it. London's hips left the couch as a spark of electricity shot through her. When he did it again, her hips bucked toward him and a loud moan left her mouth.

London bit her lip to suppress the sounds escaping when she felt his fingers move away, only to leave a trail straight to her wet slit. Wetness seeped from her as he slowly pressed two fingers into her warm center. London arched her back, spreading her legs further apart as he continued to move his fingers inside her body.

A growl resonated through the room as her eyes opened and met Kieran's gaze before closing once more. Little whimpers left her mouth as she moved her hips in time with his fingers, her body was on fire and she didn't know how much longer she would last if he kept touching her like that.

"Kieran," she gasped as he picked up the pace. Before she knew what was happening she came hard, screaming his name until her throat felt raw.

"You still have clothes on," she panted.

"We could fix that."

London began to work on the buttons to his jeans. Her fingers lightly brushed his already hard erection through his boxers until his eyes closed. His breathing told her that he was desperately trying to remain in control, or else this would end before it ever really started.

London felt her body fall back to the couch once more as Kieran's mouth hungrily covered hers. His tongue caressed hers as he groaned into her mouth. Having had enough Kieran peeled off his jeans and underwear and kicked them to the side. London's eyes widened as she stared at his very large erection.

"Do you want me to stop," Kieran asked her as he nibbled on her ear.

London slowly moved her hand down between them to grab his erection. The look she gave him urged Kieran to keep going.

"You're fucking gorgeous," he whispered as he positioned his erection at her entrance.

"Language," she gasped as she felt his throbbing member push into her body.

"Oh God!" they both moaned.

After an eternity of staying still, Kieran grabbed London's hips. As much as he wanted to move, Kieran didn't want it to end too soon. London wrapped her legs around him and used them to pull him closer to her body. London could already feel another orgasm just out of reach.

"Kieran, don't stop."

"Do you want to come Sam?"

"Yes, Sir."

"God, I love when you call me Sir," he panted slamming himself deep insider drenched center.

London's eyes closed as Kieran jackhammered into her body with no mercy. His rigid member the perfect fit for her tight core, as he slowly pulled out of her.

"Come with me," London moaned against his ear, urging him to put her out of her misery.

Strong hands grasped her arms. "Stone!"

Cobalt eyes bore down on her with an intensity so hot she wanted to look away, but something told her not to.

"London!"

"I'm sorry," she whispered before a bright glow filled the dark room as her orgasm erupted. Kieran's release followed immediately after.

His growl of pleasure mingled with her scream of ecstasy. Their breathing ragged as Kieran rolled them onto their side.

"What was that?"

"I don't know what it's called, but it's the aura all Eldites are rumored release when too much energy builds up."

"It kind of hurt."

"It kind of did," Kieran chuckled.

"What's this tattoo of?"

London's fingers traced the wheel that she knew symbolized chaos magic and moved on to the scythes on opposite sides of it.

He lazily dragged a finger across her arm, down to her ass, where he gave it a light squeeze. She giggled and nestled her head against his shoulder before the mood became serious.

"A story for another time," Kieran answered instead.

"There will be another time?"

"Definitely."

London's eyes moved away from his perfect smile. She didn't know if there was a future for them, but she couldn't help asking an impossible question.

"Why are you doing this?"

"I told the truth earlier. As much as I don't want to be attracted to you, I am. And I really do like you."

"What happens next then?"

"Let's not worry about that until the sun comes up. Deal?"

"Deal."

TWENTY

Simon passed by the same street for the third time, being careful not to be spotted. His eyes moved slowly as he surveyed everything from the brick exteriors to the people coming out of its doors. He took the same route for a few days and was surprised when he saw London carrying a suitcase to her car with Kieran.

Simon already set everything in motion, all he needed to do was collect his cash and watch as the fireworks exploded. Then he could collect Dominique and go back to being the man she remembered. He hadn't always been the man he was today. No, he was the privileged frat boy Simon Monroe.

Only his grandfather called him Wesley. He always hated Simon's mother for not making it his first name. So on paper, he was Simon Monroe, but to everyone in his line of work, he was Wes. It was easy to separate the two, but lately, he found cracks were starting to form, and he blamed London Reign.

Devereux wouldn't be happy knowing he was following London, but Wes didn't work for anyone but himself, unlike Simon. That included Georgia Rae.

The whistle that floated through the air was both menacing and catchy, any unsuspecting woman would have caught herself bobbing her head to the tune. That was how he found her; Dominique. It was through the interest she showed in him.

Wes always loved that about her, and he would love it again once he convinced her to run away with him.

Simon believed his obsession with women began the night he met Dominique. Everything about her was like setting off fireworks, from the way she walked to her smile. He had to have her. That night the two of them talked for hours and Simon knew right then that she was the girl he would marry one day.

Dominique even made him wait six months before the two consummated their relationship. She wasn't a modest girl or a prude by any means, but she was hurt in the past and she explained to Simon she wanted to make sure he was the one.

The fact she had said those words meant the world to Simon and so that night the two of them made love for the first time.

After that life was good for the two love birds. Simon worked in accounting and Dominique dreamed of owning her own business. Life was good—until it wasn't.

The first time Simon hit her was an accident, a reflex. He hadn't meant to hurt her but she was out all night with a coworker and people might think they were fucking. What would that look like to Simon and the world?

Dominique hadn't thought the same way and a fight ensued. She called him an idiot. Well, maybe not him, but she had said that way of thinking was idiotic. It was the same thing in Simon's book and when she went to walk by, he grabbed her arm and refused to let go.

One more strongly worded comment and before he knew it, Simon used the back of his hand to silence her. Yes, sound floated through the room but at least she wasn't calling him an idiot or telling him how he needed to relax.

He promised her would never hit her again, but she always did something to deserve it. That was until the last time he hit her, and she fell into the edge of the table. There was so much blood, he knew she must be dead, so he left. No need for him to lose his life too over an accident. That was until he saw her again.

She swore up and down she wasn't Dominique, but he knew different. She was trying to trick him. They all tried to trick him.

Most of his prizes didn't make it past the first night, but this one had. Once he realized London wouldn't be coming out for air anytime soon, he decided maybe it was time to check on his beloved.

The loud pounding of his steel-toed boots moved down the alley across town. He looked over his shoulder to his car, he shouldn't have parked close to the street. The drive to the warehouse took longer than he remembered.

The chains around the padlock clanged and rattled together, the key sliding in and out with ease. The iron door was hard to open like the last time he stepped foot inside. But Wes found with a little brute strength he could open anything. A rusted iron door was no exception.

Silence greeted him as he descended the narrow stairs, his eyes on his prize. Curly dark locks of hair hung down around her face, covering most of her features. The sound startled her awake, tear-stained eyes focused on him. Simon's hand reached out to caress her there, surprised when she tried to move away.

"Are you still afraid?"

When he got no response, his hand found hers, twisting them until there was tension. The whimper that escaped was music to his ears, so much so he twisted once more for good measure. Muffled screams echoed in his ears as he looked down at her almond eyes, the promise of great things to come reflected in her chocolate pools.

"I'm going to take off your gag again, ok? If you scream, bad things will happen to you. Do you understand Dominique?"

Shannon nodded her head immediately. With the gag removed from her mouth, a whimper escaped followed by a soft sob, "Please...I'm so thirsty. Can I please get water? I won't do anything, I promise," the voice croaked out.

"Where are my manners?" Simon laughed, "Of course, you can have water. I'm so forgetful sometimes," he continued to laugh at his oversight.

"Here you are, Dominique. Be careful," Simon quietly spoke in hushed tones, releasing her cuffs.

"I'm sorry," Shannon whispered back, her eyes moving to the left as she grabbed her hidden weapon. The cuffs stopped her attempt to plunge the rusted spike into Simon's leg.

"Me too," Simon replied, his voice full of remorse as he moved to grab her arm, twisting it behind her back, the other hand moving to her throat.

The feel of her smooth skin under his hands gave him a burst of energy as he began to squeeze. The struggle was minimum since she was already too weak to fight. Maybe that was a blessing in disguise.

"Fuck! Look at what you made me do, Dominque!" Simon yelled as his eyes stared down at her lifeless face.

It was too late for remorse now, he needed to figure a way to lure London away from Kieran. She was attached to him since the bowling alley. She would put up a fight, that was just the game they all played. But once she saw he was only trying to cleanse her, she'd be grateful.

Because if she stayed with Kieran Alexander, she was going to die. If Simon convinced her to stay away from Kieran, he knew she would eventually come around.

Georgia Rae left out the part about her being an Eldite when she hired Simon to kidnap London. He would never believe she was an Eldite if he didn't see it with his own eyes while spying on her. She was an abomination, but he had grown to care for her. That was why Simon came up with another way to cleanse her of the darkness that lurked within her.

Simon knew once she heard him out, London wouldn't have a problem giving up her immortality to save her damned soul.

TWENTY-ONE

London thought she would feel guiltier waking up next to Kieran. She wanted to be filled with doubt because of Simon but she couldn't muster up the emotion. Post-coital glow was all she felt in the moment.

Soft vibrating coming from her phone wiped the smile from her face instantly.

"What's wrong?"

"It's Simon. He wants to know if I made it home safely."

"A little late for that isn't it?" Kieran placed kisses along London's shoulder stopping at the base of her neck.

There was the guilt. She hadn't escaped it after all, it just needed a reminder to come barreling in guns blazing.

"He's a nice guy."

"I don't give a fuck about Simon, right now London."

"It's just—"

"What? He's a good guy? He thinks of you as a bet he can win with me."

"That's a crass thing to say. Why would you say that?"

"Because it's true. He even wanted the best man to win. He just didn't know I'm always the best."

London felt her heart skip a beat or maybe it was her holding her breath. Either way she felt like an idiot and said the first thing that came to mind.

"We can't keep doing this."

"Doing what?"

"Fucking."

"Who's the crass one now?" Kieran's face twisted into a snarl as he moved towards London.

"Kieran—"

"Call me Stone."

"I thought you hate being called that."

"I used to hate it until I heard you moan it. Now you're the only one I want to hear saying it."

Kieran's husky voice traveled straight to London's core. She didn't know when she started thinking with her vagina, but she knew it was time to start using her brain instead.

"I should be with Simon."

"But you're not. You're with me."

Part of his statement was correct. London was physically with him and if she was honest with herself, she was slowly starting to fall for his rough exterior. But it was the parts of him that she caught glimpses of that really affected her.

She hadn't committed to dating Simon. She only went on the one outing. And look how that turned out; with London on her back screaming Kieran's name.

"I'm not dating you though." London doubled down because she should be dating Simon.

"Would you like to date me? Because if we're being honest, every time I see him near you I want to break his fucking face."

"That just sounds like an if I can't have you no one can mentality, Kieran."

"What I'm saying London, is that I don't want anyone else to have you but me."

"Why?"

"You're slowly getting under my skin. So will you and your smart-ass mouth only see me for the foreseeable future, wherever that leads?"

London stayed quiet for a moment before her mouth opened say something sarcastic. Instead, all that came out was, "Yes."

Kieran's smile was breathtaking as he held up his index finger and said, "Stay right there."

The bed sagged for a moment before it bounced with his exit. London watched as Kieran left the bedroom, the sound of objects moving around causing her to laugh.

"What are you doing?"

"You'll see!" Kieran's voice was louder than it should have been followed by more clanging.

"Does that make us boyfriend and girlfriend? Do I need to tell Simon?"

"Fuck Simon," London heard from the opposite room.

"Kieran, I'm serious!" London yelled as she climbed out of bed and began putting on her clothing to follow him into the living room.

"And I heard you," Kieran answered, returning with a tray in his hands. It contained sliced limes and salt arranged beside a bottle of tequila.

"What's this?"

"Go lay back down."

"Kieran, I asked you—"

"And I said to go lay down London."

The tone of his voice gave no room for discussion. She saw the look before when he had her screaming his name over and over. This look was trouble, but London didn't dare defy him. She slowly walked toward the bed.

"Take off your clothes, first. I didn't tell you to get dressed."

"Kieran," she whispered.

"Kieran says get undressed."

With the nod of her head, London began removing her clothing starting with her top and slowly working her way to her shorts.

"What do you want me to do now?"

Her inability to hide her fear and arousal was evident by the way Kieran's eyes moved over her naked body.

"Climb on the bed and close your eyes."

"You know I hate that."

"Trust me," he stated confidently. A simple nod was all London could muster as she did what she was told.

"I tried staying away at first," Kieran whispered in her ear before he took her earlobe between his teeth. When he heard her moan he let go and whispered, "God, you're beautiful."

Before London could respond, his mouth covered hers hungrily. His hands slid down her body grasping her breast. She quivered from the attention he was giving her body. His fingers gently massaged her breast and lightly pinched her nipples, which made her arch up to meet his advances.

A few moments later, she felt cold liquid touch her stomach, quickly replaced by the warmth of what could only be his tongue. The heat that she felt from his mouth was unbearable. London wanted to urge him take them off and thrust them into her.

London gasped and began to writhe as his tongue assaulted her body, moving from her belly button to her heaving breasts.

"Don't move," he stated firmly.

Her body ached to have him inside her. But instead, he went back to worshipping her breast. London whimpered as her body begged to move against his advances. But every time she moved her body to lift her hips toward his mouth, she received a warning smack to her inner thigh, inches away from her wet center, followed by a soft kiss to ease the sting.

The slow lick trailed down to her calf before making the painful ascent back to her sore thigh.

London's breath came out as moans as she tried to focus on staying calm. All that became impossible once she felt him flick her clit.

Her body arched toward him as he did it again and again. It was almost as if her body was betraying her because what she wanted it to do was stay still. He wanted to make her beg for release. And for the first time, she didn't mind at all.

London's hands clenched her sheets as an orgasm rocked her body. Even as the convulsions started to subside, she was racked with yet another one. Kieran was relentless as he continued to lick at her sex. London could feel his fingers digging into her body as he held her tightly to him. He tried as hard as he could to keep her still, but the more he licked at her center, the wilder she became.

"Stone—"

"Yes baby," he whispered as he climbed up her body.

London could feel his erection rubbing against her wet slit. She started to smile but, instead, sucked in a breath as he rubbed his erection against her again. Kieran's eyes burned into hers as he deliberately shifted once more, caressing her with his body.

London clutched at his shoulders as she tried to press her body into him. She cried out as he pulled back a little and surged forward, allowing his erection to fill her. Her body tensed and quivered as he bent his head to kiss away the rest of her tension.

Kieran withdrew and surged forward again, London's nails digging into his back, urging him to continue. He immediately covered her mouth with his as he began thrusting faster. London concentrated on meeting his thrusts, her body filled with pleasure.

"God!"

"That's it. Come for me, baby."

London bit into his shoulder to keep from screaming out too loud. She clenched at his manhood as she came hard, and within seconds he was moaning her name as he came inside her. The white glow was forgotten as they came down from their high.

Kieran rolled her so she lay on top of him. His fingers ran along her arms as he placed kisses along her collarbone.

"We should do that more often."

"I agree."

"Is it bad that I still feel a little guilty?"

"You've been feeling guilty? About what?"

London turned her head away from Kieran. She didn't want him to see her face when she told him what was really bothering her. She already knew his stance on the subject and looking at him while she said it again wouldn't make it better.

"Part of me just feels like I've fucked up. And I keep thinking, what have I done?"

"You made a decision to keep fucking me. That's what you did." There was an unmistakable chuckle that forced London to turn towards him.

"Kieran—"

"And I fucked you back," he finished.

"But what about Simon?"

"You didn't fuck Simon tonight, London. He's not here. I am."

"My fear is that I have to go into work tomorrow and see him."

"Do you want me to fire him?"

"No!" London gasped as she felt his body move away from hers.

"Because I will."

"No. Please don't do that."

"Look London. This is new for both of us. Let's just play it by ear."

"Right. Play it by ear."

"Just know that your pussy has my name on it now. Not Simon's. If he touches you, I won't be responsible for my actions."

"Really, Kieran. You're already threatening him?"

"Yes," he answered leaning in to kiss her, "I am."

And just like that she had entered into a committed relationship with her boss and the man who technically was still blackmailing her. Although, he hadn't used any of the information he had. In the end she might like being possessed by Kieran Alexander after all.

She just hoped that he didn't break her heart in the process.

TWENTY-TWO

London felt out of place as soon as she stepped into Renegades for her shift. She took advantage of the story that she was sick and stayed in bed all week with Kieran whenever she could. Did they all know she was fucking the boss? No one looked at her with disgust or anger. That was a good sign, right?

"Lonny," a chorus of voices rang out in unison.

"Yes?"

"We were so worried. We heard you had the flu. Are you okay?"

"You did? From whom?"

"Me."

She would know that voice anywhere.

"Mrs. Reign, can I have a word with you in my office?"

"Good luck girl," she heard one of her coworkers whisper with a pat on the back.

London followed behind Kieran until they were out of sight. His fingers laced with hers as they walked to his office. London knew what he wanted. She wanted it too, but now was not the time to get caught with their pants down.

"I don't know if this is a good idea."

"Talking?"

"Is that what we are going to do back here? Talk?"

"In a manner of speaking."

Kieran bridged the gap between the two of them and placed a soft kiss on London's lips once the door closed. His eyes closed the moment London's arms wrapped around his neck. A moan vibrated through her body as he stoked the fire within her.

The kiss lasted a few moments before Kieran pulled away from her. She needed him too much to let him be away from her for even a second.

London plastered her body to his as her arms snaked around his neck once more, her breast pressed against his chest. Their softness was a perfect contrast to his firm body. Kieran's hand wrapped around London's waist as he pulled her to him. Both were close and yet miles away.

"Hands on the desk," Kieran whispered as he turned her slowly toward the large mahogany piece of furniture.

A smile covered London's face as she complied without question.

"Such a good fucking girl," he growled as his hand made contact with her ass.

The yelp that followed was drowned out by the sound check down the hall. There was no mistake, this moment was made for them.

"Count them."

Those were the only words London got before Kieran's hand met her ass once more. She didn't know why, but she yelled out the number one afraid of what would happen if she didn't.

Each following smack was just as hard until he got to the number twenty-nine and paused.

"What number are we on?"

"Twenty-nine—Sir," she added quickly.

"Okay, we have two more—you know, one to grow on."

London braced herself for what was to come until he rubbed her sore ass. She wasn't expecting his fingers to venture further south until they reached the junction of her thighs.

"Kieran—"

"So fucking good," she heard Kieran murmur to himself as one, then two fingers entered London's pussy.

"Oh, god."

"Close enough." The chuckle traveled to London's ears and faded away on a moan. She never fucked on a desk. And she wasn't about to now. She almost cried as both fingers were removed and nothing inserted in their place.

"Thank you for your time, Mrs. Reign."

He wasn't serious, was he?

London wanted to scream but she knew that this was her punishment for lying about her birthday weeks ago. She would suck it up and let Kieran have his fun, but by the end of the night, she was going to have some fun of her own.

"Is there anything else?" London asked, glad to play along with whatever role-play this was.

"No, thank you, Mrs. Reign. Close the door on the way out."

London did as she was told and walked back toward the music. The closer she got the louder the noise became until she opened the door.

The day quickly morphed into night as the club opened. Within hours Renegades was packed wall to wall with half-naked bodies. London couldn't tell if they were there for Adarai or worked next door at the Garden. The only thing she was certain of was that Jaxon could throw one hell of a party.

The tenth annual mascot contest was a hit. The winner got drinks at happy hour prices for an hour.

"It's Adarai bitch!" London overheard an enthusiastic patron scream, followed by more yelling. The crash in the background followed by a slew of expletives was exactly what London didn't need.

"God," she huffed under her breath as she met security near a drunk young woman.

"I'm good," the young woman slurred before falling back to the ground.

"Can you make sure she gets a cab or someone can come to get her?" London asked the replacement guard. Normally Mason would be at an event like this to add support, but instead, they were one person short for one of their busiest nights of the year.

"Will do."

"Thanks," the smile she gave was genuine as she turned and walked into Simon.

"Ow. If you wanted to see me again there was no reason to injure me."

London could tell it was supposed to be a joke, but all she felt was guilt for leading him on when she knew there was no future for them.

"If only," London awkwardly joked.

"Actually, we never got to finish our date and I remember you saying you'd give me a rain check."

London's first instinct was to say no, but then her eyes caught Kieran's as he walked from the back.

Sorry, Simon.

"I'd love to do that. Wanna get out of here now. We can go—" London was unable to finish her sentence before Kieran was beside her, his hand pressed firmly against her back.

"Come with me."

"Is this important, Sir? Simon and I were just leaving."

"It's life and death."

"You should go," Simon answered, not allowing London time to make Kieran squirm a little.

"Thanks for understanding Monroe."

"Anytime Stone," she heard Simon counter.

The ride home was quiet, the only words uttered from Kieran, "Get out."

London's eyes moved around the foyer drifting up to the chandelier above her head. Its colorful prisms reflected onto the surface of the walls. She remembered a time when she would have hated being commanded to go anywhere with Kieran.

Strong arms wrapped around her. London took refuge in Kieran, allowing all of her body heat to transfer to him. The smell of sandalwood and her lavender body wash drifted up to her nose.

"Close your eyes," he whispered against the curve of her neck, giving it a quick nip. A moan left London's lips as she did what he asked and closed her eyes.

A few seconds passed without any sound, the silence deafening, except for the sound of her breathing. Heat radiated from Kieran's body as he held her to him tightly. But just as she focused on the warmth, it was gone.

"Kieran?"

A few seconds passed before she heard his voice again. "Open them."

London's brown eyes opened to find that the foyer was darker than before. The sound of movement behind her forced her to turn. "What are you doing?"

"What does it look like?" Kieran's voice came from the opposite direction she was looking. London swung around only to find he wasn't there.

"I don't know" she whispered. "Playing a game?"

"What do you think we're playing?" he asked, his laughter made London blush. She had no idea what they were playing.

"To be honest, it reminds me of a game of cat and mouse."

"Can you guess which one you are?"

London didn't answer his question. She stood rooted to the same spot, listening for any sound that seemed out of place, hoping to pick up some kind of noise.

When the lights came back on, London saw Kieran at the end of the hall. The look in his eyes said he wanted to devour her.

"Run," he growled loudly.

London yelped and did as she was told. Her legs moved faster than she knew they could. The sound of his footsteps getting closer as she ran upstairs and stopped. She would get caught if she went to the most obvious spot.

Her indecision led to her capture as strong arms grabbed London by the waist.

"Fuck."

"Want to play another game with me?" Kieran husked against her ear, nipping at it with his teeth.

The only thing she could manage was a nod. "I can't hear you."

"Ye—yes. Yes, I want to play another game with you," she whimpered when he pulled her hair tightly in his fist. The sudden pain that shot through her scalp sent an electric current straight to her wet center.

"I don't think I heard you correctly."

"Yes, Sir!" London moaned loudly through the pain.

"Great answer." He smiled letting go of her hair. "Follow me."

London nodded her head and began to follow him into the bedroom. "Lay on the bed," he ordered sternly with no room for argument.

Kieran slowly lifted London's shirt over her head, inch by inch he slowly exposed the smooth skin that lay beneath it. She couldn't help but notice his eyes never left her body. Her red lace bra hugged her breast tightly. London watched Kieran lower his head and flick her hard nipple through the fabric.

London couldn't help the gasp that escaped or the moan that followed. He brought his attention to the other nipple and captured it in his mouth, tugging lightly at it as he softly flicked it with his tongue. When another moan escaped her mouth Kieran stood with her still plastered to his body and turned to lay her gently on the bed.

London's hair was wildly splayed over the bed, breast heaving rapidly from the passion that she felt. Kieran shifted his body down hers, stopping at the button of her shorts, his eyes found hers again as he slowly unbuttoned them and dragged the zipper down.

"Raise your hips," Kieran whispered.

She did exactly as he asked and slowly lifted her hips, once London did as he commanded, Kieran peeled the shorts down her thighs until they were at her feet, pulling them over her feet slowly, kissing her calves as he did.

London could feel the moisture seeping through her panties and wondered if Kieran noticed. She felt the weight of her shorts vanish only to be replaced by the feel of his lips on the inside of her thigh. Another moan left her body, as she tangled her fingers in his hair. She never experienced anything like this. The sensations slowly creeping up her body were catching her off guard.

Passing her wet sex, Kieran moved over London and stared into her eyes again. He captured her lips with his own, and London felt him groan when her tongue darted into his mouth.

She could feel his erection pressing against her completely soaked panties, her hands clutched his shoulders as the kiss started to grow more demanding. She was now grinding her hips against him trying to get as close to him as possible. Kieran broke their kiss and buried his head in the crook of her neck, before moving on to kiss her shoulder. His hands cupped her breasts as he lightly palmed them, letting his thumb stroke them to life again.

He used his index and middle finger as he playfully pretended to walk down her body. The laugh that escaped was breathless, and he couldn't help but smile as well. His fingers came to rest at the top of the apex of her thighs. Kieran allowed the two fingers to slowly slide down between her legs where they found her clit and began to massage it.

London's hips left the bed as a spark of electricity shot through her, his fingers moving her underwear to the side. London bit her lip to suppress the sounds escaping when she felt his fingers move away only to lightly trail over her wet slit. Wetness seeped from her as he slowly pressed two fingers into her warm center. London arched her back, spreading her legs further apart as he continued to move his fingers inside her womanhood.

A growl resonated through the room as Kieran gazed down at what he was doing to her. London's eyes had closed and she was making little whimpering sounds as she moved her hips in time with his fingers. Her body was on fire and she didn't know how much longer she would last if he kept touching her like that.

"You still have clothes on," she panted, then a small smile crept across her face and she said, "We'll just have to fix that now won't we."

With the flick of her hand, London began to work on the button to Kieran's jeans.

"Take them off."

He did exactly as she told him, moving the material down his hips at a painstakingly slow rate. When they were past his thighs he let go and she watched them pool around his feet. Her hands reached for him and she lightly brushed his already hard erection through his boxers. Kieran's eyes immediately closed and he tried desperately to calm himself or else all this would end before it ever really started.

Kieran maneuvered London onto the bed again, his tongue caressing hers as he groaned into her mouth. When they broke apart, both were panting, staring into each other's eyes.

"Do you want me to stop?" Kieran asked her as he nibbled on her ear, he had sensed the fear she had and wanted to make sure he was doing the right thing. The heat that arose told him everything he needed to know. She was ready for him.

"I love you," London whispered.

"What?"

"I'm sorry. I don't know where that came from. I—"

"Babe, I'm home," a voice came from the doorway.

"What the fuck?" Kieran jumped up, looking behind him at the leggy blonde in nothing but underwear. "Candy?"

"Babe? Do you know her?" London asked as she scrambled to cover her body.

"Is this her, she's cute. I'm totally down for that threesome, she's exactly our style."

"Kieran, who is this? What is she talking about?"

"I have no idea what she's talking about!" Kieran yelled.

"Babe, you don't remember our conversation about finding a third? You thought it would be hot if we added a little spice to the relationship. I wasn't expecting a Black girl though. How kinky."

"Excuse you!"

"Did he pull your hair? Maybe spank your ass a little. He's been reading up about bondage and all those other taboo things, like that one movie."

"Kieran?"

"London don't believe any of that. She's fucking lying."

"Stone, baby, why would you say that?"

"Stone?" Kieran watched as London grabbed her clothes and began pulling them on.

"London, don't."

"Oh, so you're protecting her now? So you do know her?"

"Yes, but it's not like that."

"So you've never mentioned a threesome with her?"

"I haven't even seen her in weeks."

"Wow, weeks, that's so long," London laughed, "Well you can both go straight to hell."

London spoke in a low voice, trying her best not to cry. She wouldn't give them the satisfaction of seeing her break. "I should have known."

"Sam."

"Don't—" The last thing she saw was the woman named Candy placing her arms around Kieran. London knew it was too good to be true, there was no such thing as love, just pain, and destruction. Her reflection showed an orange glow as her eyes matched the rage she felt inside, static electricity crackling from her fingertips.

If she wanted him, she could have him.

London Reign didn't need a man to complete her or teach her to control her abilities. She didn't need Kieran.

She would rather burn.

TWENTY-THREE

Confusion washed over Kieran as he watched his former date step into the room spewing lies. He didn't blame London for bailing on him. She confided in him and now there was a woman claiming to already be his girlfriend.

How did she even know where he lived? Better yet, how did she get into his house? Kieran didn't know what was going on but when he felt Candy embrace him, his body instantly went into defense mode.

"What are you doing?" Kieran yelled as he pushed Candy away.

"What you asked me to do."

There was no way in hell Kieran asked some stranger to come into his home and derail his life. The crazy thing was she looked as if she believed her lie.

"We had one date. One date that ended horribly. Why would I want to see you again at all?"

"It wasn't all bad," she rationalized.

"So you just showed up here and told my—"

Kieran paused with the word girlfriend on the tip of his tongue. He had never had a serious girlfriend. Sure, he had several conquests, but none of them ever had a title.

"Candy, how do you know where I live?"

"You can find pretty much anything online these days," She gave a smile that said she was being coy.

"Not mine."

"I thought you would be happy to see me."

"And why would I be happy to see you? We only had one date." Kieran was fed up with her crazy rationalization. He asked the same question again, "How did you know where I live?"

The boom of Kieran's voice made Candy jump. Fear was never a motivator for Kieran when it came to getting answers. Fear was simply a means to an end when wholesome interrogation techniques failed. He would never use Cerbi techniques on an Undesirable, but for a moment he thought about it for Candy.

Candy the stripper.

"Wes said to go for it, to show you what you should have. I'm what you should have, not some waitress."

"You decided to listen to a friend and stalk me?"

"Wes isn't a friend. I met him a couple of weeks ago."

"Oh great. You listened to a fucking stranger. Solid idea, Candy."

"And you remember my name this time," she boasted. "Besides, you should know Wes. He works for you."

Not only was she a liar but she was also bat shit crazy. Kieran would know if someone named Wes worked for him. There was no one by that name on his payroll.

"I can guarantee you no one by that name works for me!" Kieran yelled back, his octave growing.

"He said his friends call him Simon."

At that moment it all started to make sense. Simon was in it to win it. Well, Kieran wasn't about to let him take London away. Not without a fight.

"Tell me everything you talked to Simon about."

London's feet felt like lead as they took her step by step toward the exit. Tears streamed down her face along with small gasps of air. She struggled to run and use her phone simultaneously. London knew she was a fool to ever let Kieran trick her into believing he had feelings for her.

She knew from the beginning their relationship consisted of him blackmailing her and eventually sex. The sound of her name from the top of the stairs passed over her head. Her feet quickening their steps; she needed to get out and fast.

"Whoa, slow down before you hurt someone." Mason stood at the door poised to open it with a key. "What's got you in such a hurry? And why are you coming from Kieran's place?"

"Ask your man whore of a friend. Unless you already know. Was Kieran's house off limits? Only supposed to be confined to the guest house, huh?"

"I just meant because it's the middle of the day. Shit, what happened?"

"I don't have time, Mason. I just need to get out of here. I need—I need to leave."

London tried her best to hold her composure. Her voice cracked just as she noticed the fact that the house had gone silent. She knew what that meant for the two of them. She didn't want to be inside when the moaning began. London wasn't that big of a glutton that she'd punish herself any longer.

"Okay. Let's go. We'll stop by the club."

"I don't want to go to Renegades."

"Not Renegades. It's a club owned by a friend. Not exactly what you would imagine, so keep an open mind.

"I don't know—"

"You look like you could use a drink," Mason interrupted.

"Sure. I could use a drink," London whispered as she let Mason move her toward his car

There wasn't much to say on the way to Mason's friend. And Mason must have known the drill because he didn't try to initiate a conversation. How many of Kieran's conquests had he consoled this way?

London wasn't naïve enough to think he hadn't been with anyone at all, but to have it thrown in her face was a completely different story. They hadn't started out friends, but she thought the past couple of weeks meant something. She was wrong.

"We're here."

"Obsidian." The red neon sign adorned the front of the building. In front of the establishment was a man who was dressed in a black button up and black slacks with the sign that read *valet* attached to a podium.

The luxury car that pulled up to him looked more expensive than anything she saw pull into a club. The woman who got out was thin and smelled of money even from the moving car.

With the nod of his head, Mason continued to drive past the man and down into a parking garage.

Where had he taken her?

"I don't know about this Mason."

"Don't worry, no one's here right now. Plus, it's the only place I know with decent booze. No offense to Jaxon and Kieran."

"Fuck Kieran."

After a few seconds, Mason opened his door, "Fair enough."

The parking lot was empty which was a relief for London. She didn't want to be around a lot of people.

"Where are we going?"

"Not far," Mason answered as he walked to a single elevator and tapped in a four-digit code. Weird.

"Come with me and try not to judge too much."

"Who says I'll judge this place."

"Everyone does the first time," was the only thing Mason said as the doors to the elevator closed.

A sea of bodies greeted London and Mason once the elevator doors opened. Half-naked bodies moved around freely amongst the dark purple and black. Obsidian was definitely not the same on the inside as it appeared on the outside.,

"What in the world?"

"Exactly." Mason laughed as he led London towards a door that looked like something out of a vampire musical.

"This is empty?!"

"Knock knock!" Mason yelled while opening the door.

"Doc, my man!"

"Dom, what's up? I wasn't expecting to actually see you here."

"Well it is my club. Got a call that some of the Scooby gang were going at it, refusing to leave."

"Scooby gang?"

"Yeah. My way of saying goodie two shoes. They don't really fit in a place like this. Kinda like you, hello." Dom smiled giving one of the best thousand-watt smiles. "But you look like you could be some trouble too."

"Off limits, Dominique. She's Kieran's."

"I'm no one's, especially Kieran's. Kieran has a girlfriend—Candy."

"I can guarantee Kieran doesn't have a girlfriend, he's not the settling down type."

"Thanks a lot, Dom," Mason growled as his eyes shifted toward London.

"Good to know," London laughed as she walked toward the exit. She knew all of the things Mason told her were lies and she was still willing to give Kieran the benefit of the doubt. Her lungs burned as she tried her hardest to catch her breath. The heat London thought she had under control was back with a vengeance.

"I just need to get out of here," London said as she ordered an Uber to take her anywhere.

TWENTY-FOUR

London's head moved from left to right to make sure she wasn't being followed. She took an Uber from Renegades and went to the park Kieran asked her to meet him at. Once she realized she was following her feelings back to Kieran she ordered another Uber to take her to Bean Me Up Java Co., only to find it was closed.

Of course, her Uber driver had already left. Plus, to add insult to injury her phone was dead.

"Perfect."

Lucky for her she wasn't far from a gas station and could call her mother to pick her up. It was about time she let Ruby know what was happening. She had allowed her emotions to take over in a way she had not foreseen, and now she was paying the price. It took a lot of effort to keep from burning everything she came into contact with down to the ground.

London took the quickest way she could think of; the alley between Beam Me Up Java Co. and its competitor Dark Side Grind. Alleys were notorious for being dangerous. London saw enough scary movies to know that once someone went down an alley they were as good as dead.

However, at this moment she'd take possible death over calling anyone from Renegades and hearing more about Kieran and his lies. London's hatred of them both was much higher than her love for him.

With her train of thought fixated on her recent behavior, London couldn't believe that she allowed him to fool her, all in the name of love. A twisted kind of love that began with blackmail and ended in heartache.

Kieran played her.

The frigid air attacked London's lungs as her breathing became erratic. She just needed to get home and forget about the day. This part of Terra wasn't known for its cold weather but lately, it was all anyone got. And now her insides matched the outside.

"Hey, watch it!"

London's shoulder collided with something hard, her eyes moving up to see a person standing in front of her. His face turned up in a scowl as she tried to move around him. His movements mimicked hers and prevented her from walking around him.

"I don't want any trouble. I'm just trying to get home."

"Well, maybe you should watch where you're going, bitch."

"I'll remember that next time," London murmured as she took another step to the side.

The man matched her once more, "Are you trying to be smart with me?"

"Look, I don't have time for this," she huffed turning her back to him, her intention to walk away when she felt a hand grab her by the neck.

"No one disrespects me like that, bitch," the man's voice laced with anger and malice as he pulled her down the street toward an alley. She knew that was where people died and she escaped one only to be dragged back toward one, but not without a fight. London's hands dug into the side of the man's arms, his scream just what she needed to facilitate a getaway.

"Help! Someone help!"

"You're gonna pay for that, you fucking bitch."

It was then London paid attention to him, his muscle shirt and backward hat screamed douche. She wasn't sure if he was dressed in a costume or if this was his everyday attire. All she knew was if she didn't do something she'd be another statistic on the news.

London's heels dug into the ground, her hands tingling as her body began to warm up. Not again, she thought as her attacker tossed her to the ground. She was going to die and she was having a hot flash, perfect.

"I'll teach you to disrespect me." The douche scowled, his hands fumbling with his belt.

"NO—"

The scream was cut short as the man fell to the ground. His body convulsed on the ground as electricity shot through him. Had she done that?

"London?"

London's eyes moved up to see a familiar face running in her direction. "Simon?"

"Oh my god, London? Are you okay?" Simon rushed to her side, making no effort to get around the man lying on the ground, stepping on his crotch in the process.

"I...I don't know."

"Kieran had me come find you. He tracked your phone to this area until your signal disappeared."

"It died," London explained as she tried her best to ignore the man laying a few feet from them.

"And why didn't Kieran come himself?"

"He's with some chick. They went into his office so I don't know what happened but it sounded heated."

Unwanted tears fell down London's cheeks one by one.

"It's okay."

"Thank you," she sobbed, tears of relief streamed down her face. London wasn't an idiot. If Simon hadn't come along who knows what would have happened to her?

"What are you doing out here by yourself at night coming out of an alley?"

"I was heading to a gas station," London responded. Although it was not the entire reason, it was also not a lie.

She didn't have the energy to come up with a story to cover all the other lies she was hiding. Instead, she only wanted to go home and take a much-needed shower.

"I have my car. I'm not letting you walk at this time of night."

London wanted to tell Simon no. She didn't want company, all she wanted was the pain she felt to disappear, but it was her fault. She went into the situation with the realization everything Kieran did had ulterior motives.

"No, I'll be fine—"

"I insist," Simon pressed, "After what I just saw I'd hate myself if something were to happen to you and I just let you leave without at least seeing you home."

"Yeah. Okay," London finally agreed to allow his hand to capture hers.

Moments later London's eyes closed and she allowed herself to relax. She thought of a world that was fractured. Her world. There was no way to fix it except to find out if what Kieran said was true, her dad was a well-respected Collector within the Cerbi community. She allowed a good lay to distract her and make her think of words like love.

What did she know about love?

Nothing, that was what she knew about love.

London's eyes opened to find her surroundings were unfamiliar. The buildings that stood against the darkness were rundown and decrepit.

"Simon, where are we?"

"Just taking a shortcut."

"This is a weird shortcut; I've never seen any of these buildings."

"Just gotta make a pit stop first and then I'll take you home," Simon answered while pulling into a different alley.

"Simon?"

"It's a new spot for the club I've been scouting for the guys. I think I dropped my wallet here. It'll be quick, I promise."

"I'll stay here while you get it," London offered, feeling a little uneasy again.

"Nonsense, come with me."

"I'd like to go home, Simon. You can come back here during the day."

"Are you scared?" He laughed.

"Yes," London whispered so low even she almost didn't hear herself.

"I don't understand."

London didn't either. The thought pushed at her as she made a deal to open the door and run. She didn't know how long she would have before all hell broke loose, but something wasn't right. If Simon was with the Tribunal, then they were gunning for her to disappear. Add to the fact Kieran was no longer a distraction for her and it all became increasingly clear.

"You're going to kill me, aren't you?"

"Why do you say that?"

"I don't know."

"You don't know or you don't want to say?" Simon asked turning in her direction.

"Both."

"God, you really are a stupid bitch."

"What did you —?"

"It wasn't hard getting close to you. I mean." Simon paused for a moment to point at his face, "Look at me."

"I knew there was some craziness going on but after following you for a while I've seen it's far more sinister than I ever imagined."

"Simon—I thought we were friends," London sobbed as a tear fell. She really needed to stop crying. They didn't deserve her tears.

"We aren't."

If she ever doubted the devil was in the details, she didn't now. The Devil was definitely here. And his name was Simon Monroe.

"Why?"

Her question was cut off as a cloth was placed against her face. London struggled for as long as she could until her body went limp. The words, "I got her," were the last thing London heard before her world went black.

TWENTY-FIVE

Soot wrapped around her body like the aftermath of an atomic bomb, filling the air with darkness. A loud thud followed by a groan floated through the cinderblock cell. Her body hit the ground with more force than she had expected. The stone wall stopped the momentum, in the same way, it stops a car.

Harsh whispers drifted toward her sore body, each word mingling with the rhythmic dripping into the rusted bucket in the corner of the room. The small object reeked of urine and something she couldn't quite put her finger on. Each whiff slowly suffocated her as she began to cough.

London wasn't sure if this was due to the smell or hitting a literal wall. Even now she didn't want to think of what her life had become.

Soft echoes interrupted her thoughts as she finally took in one last haggard breath. The remaining charcoal pollutant wafted through the small cell window until there was only an ashen fog. Her arm jerked above her head as the crack of bones caused the man before her to smile.

Even now she tried to stifle the scream that threatened to leave her throat. She could hear the gurgling rise from nowhere and everywhere at the same time. Music to his ears she thought. And while his orders had been not to touch her, London gathered he rationalized that a broken wrist didn't constitute touching.

"Be happy it was only your wrist and not a rib. Those are much more deadly."

Cold metal circled her wrist, locking in place with an ominous click, the sound deafening. Tears pooled, unshed as she lifted her eyes toward the broken limb. The same limb that now wore beautiful scars.

The bone was barely contained by her skin, threatening to burst through at any second with the wrong movement. A lonely tear finally escaped as London lowered her head. She had left Kieran without a word of where she would be going and her phone was dead.

"Incendius."

"Trying to use your magic on me you abomination? Well, it won't work. I spoke to some people and got myself something some protection." Simon moved his shirt collar down to show a necklace with a metal amulet attached. She knew that symbol, it looked exactly like Kieran's tattoo."

"Where did you get that?"

"Doesn't matter. What matters is I had this symbol painted on every door and wall. You're stuck here with me."

"Why are you doing this?"

"For money of course. I would get my reward and hand you over, but after I saw what you could do, I figure I could get way more over an extended period. People don't love hush money, but I do."

"I don't know what you mean?"

"You're an Eldite." Simon smirked.

"I don't know what you think you saw."

"You electrocuted someone with your bare hands." There was no hesitation in the answer spoken from Simon.

"So you were following me?"

"Good thing I did too, right? That perv was going to try and have his way with you. Attack you! But I stopped it."

"You did," London saw enough horror movies to know that sometimes the killer just needed his ego stroked.

"Once I saw where you went after Candy showed up, I knew I had to get you alone."

"Obsidian?"

"She was hiding in plain sight the whole time."

"Candy?"

"No. Dominique. She always wanted something of her own. And Obsidian is her favorite stone. Beautiful. . . just like her."

London's eyes moved past Simon's head. Play along, she told herself, just play along.

"How'd you know where to find me?"

Emerald orbs looked at her with disgust, "We established I followed you. Keep up, London."

"Did you pay that girl Candy to make it look like she was dating Kieran?"

"Stroke of genius right? I was going to kill her but she proved to be useful."

Now London sat among dirt and filth as she looked down at purple bruises that began to form. Bruising on her skin was no easy feat, but with the job, Simon had done earlier London wasn't surprised all the manhandling hadn't caused more.

"Be a good girl now," Simon growled pulling out a syringe from his pocket.

What's that for?"

"Something the witch said would help keep you agreeable," he answered removing the cap.

The pinch hurt less than what was injected in her arm. Then Simon turned his back and walked toward the entrance. The loud click of the door locking signaled that he was gone, leaving behind the only thing London needed now more than ever.

Hope.

The sound of her cell door opened slowly with a thud. Boots stomped against the floor and sent shockwaves beneath her body. The muted impact of leather soles struck the concrete with a force she had come to know as determination. London's body involuntarily moved toward the corner.

The links rattled with shuffle that her feet made. Pain shot through her wrist quickly radiating toward her shoulder. She was sure in the process of breaking her bones, she managed to dislocate her shoulder. The aftermath of being thrown into a solid brick wall.

As defiant as she could be, London knew now was not one of those times. A pudgy body moved down into focus of her making his presence known. A man she never saw before glared back at her with something that reminded her of lust. His hand slowly moved toward her face to make contact with her cheek.

"Shh," the raspy voice whispered to her, a whimper the only response capable of leaving her body. The look on his face never once changed even as his eyes moved slowly over her torn clothing and bruised body.

"Now you be a good girl, and you won't get hurt."

Coarse fingers squeezed her cheeks causing her mouth to pucker up. The stench of alcohol drifted toward her nose mingled with the smell of death. His rotten teeth were on full display as he moved his face closer to hers. London squirmed against the hand trying her best to get away even with the shackle placed generously around her wrist. The palm of his hand was the only reward for disobeying him.

"What did I just say?" he hissed, allowing copious amounts of spittle to fly, hitting her face. His palm once again squeezed her cheeks as her head pushed against the stone wall behind her.

"Bitch!"

The inebriated man stumbled back to his feet, swaying as his hands quickly fumbled with the buckle of his belt. "I'll teach you to move away from me," he sneered, releasing his zipper, and lowering his pants down his legs. Coarse tufts of hair pushed away from his body at the base of his manhood before he covered it with his hand.

"Raphael, stop!" Came a panicked voice from behind him.

"What?" he asked looking behind him with a smile on his face. "You want her first?"

"Don't you know who that is?" the newcomer balked.

"Just some bitch that needs to be taught a lesson." Raphael laughed taking another step toward London. Only this time a growl stopped him in his tracks. The kind of sound that was guttural and come from the depths of one's soul.

"What, Eric?!"

Eric moved forward grabbing London's attacker and throwing his body toward the cell door. The differences between the two were day and night. Eric was slightly shorter than Raphael, his blond hair a grave contrast to his chestnut eyes. But the one big difference that London noticed was their expression. Eric looked terrified.

"Fuck it. I'll find someone else," Raphael cursed, trying his best to stand tall all the while pulling his pants up. The determination still burning hot in his eyes.

"You won't get off that easy," London heard him shout past Eric as he moved toward the stairs.

The clanging of the door once again boomed within the small confines of the room, leaving her in the dark once more.

TWENTY-SIX

Georgia Rae rolled over in her king-sized bed. Sleep eluded her for the second night in a row, her thoughts quickly returning to her conversation with Eve. Georgia Rae's anxiety was the strongest it had ever been as night turned into dawn.

Birds chirped their cheerful song outside her window, each one unaware of how close she was to snapping. Today was the big day, London's thirtieth birthday. Rumors spread through the Tribunal that something worse than a Shift had taken place. That there was an Eldite in their midst.

The only problem with that theory was Georgia Rae already knew where the Eldite was being held. It looked suspicious when she contacted Wes again for the third time behind the Tribunal's back. Eve hadn't accused her of anything criminal, but Georgia Rae saw the wheels turning. Khaiv Rexton was finally starting to put two and two together.

But it was too late to worry about the consequences. Greatness was measured in the actions of others and Georgia Rae wanted to be the greatest. The alarm on her phone blared its generic symphony of noises, begging her to put it out of its misery. Instead, the sound sent her back to a time she had wished to forget but forced herself to relive. If she forgot, Maxwell would truly be dead, just another forgotten casualty in a war long forgotten by time.

Georgia Rae's eyes glanced at her notifications finally as she allowed her thoughts to refocus. She had one missed call along with voice messages. One of them better be from Wes. Georgia Rae left him multiple messages instructing him of the change of plans. He needed to contact her immediately. That could explain the call.

Without looking at who the call was from, Georgia Rae clicked play and was surprised by the voice on the other end.

"She's been retrieved. I'll text you the address. Meet me at the agreed upon time. Don't be late," were the only words spoken before the line went dead.

"Finally!" Georgia Rae exclaimed loudly. Her demure sophisticated act flew out the window to join her annoying avian choir.

Georgia Rae tried to decide what her next move should be. Wes already informed her of London's capture, now she just had to carry out her plans. She left out the part where she needed someone to help her extract some of London's blood in the hopes of making an elixir or drug that could transfer abilities.

Now was the time Georgia Rae had prayed for. She had even spent days trying to get in touch with her daughter, but she always sent it to voicemail. She didn't blame her. She had a lot going on at the moment. That was why Georgia Rae needed to get to London and fast if she wanted to ensure her plan went off without a hitch.

With the phone still nestled in her hand, Georgia Rae pressed one button and allowed the cold surface to rest against her shoulder and ear.

"I'll be there in two hours."

Silence followed for a brief second and then the silent click of the phone signaled Wes heard her loud and clear. Georgia Rae knew she needed to alert the Tribunal of the new development, and she would but only after she got what she needed first. Georgia Rae was sure she could figure out a way to spin the story to her liking, one way or another she was going to come out of this smelling like roses.

"Amelia, make sure the rest of the staff is prepared to receive us when we get back," Georgia Rae barked at her assistant.

"Yes, ma'am."

"And make sure Dr. Jenkins is here when we get back. I'm gonna need her expertise."

"Of course, ma'am," Amelia nodded before making her exit to ensure all of Georgia Rae's demands were met.

After Amelia departed, anxiety gripped Georgia Rae, and she knew what needed to happen. With a heavy heart, she picked up the phone and hit a different number, her speed dial getting more of a workout than Georgia Rae herself. Ringing trilled in her ear as she listened to the soft voice of a woman on the other end.

"What?"

"Eve, I know where she is. What do you want me to do?"

"Do nothing. Where is she?"

Georgia Rae knew she shouldn't alert the Collector, but she needed plausible deniability. And deep down she knew Khaiv didn't want her brought before the Tribunal. Not yet. "I'll text you the address."

"And make sure she's unharmed."

Georgia Rae's silence was the only answer the other party needed as they disconnected the call.

"Where the fuck is the car!"

Georgia Rae moved through her fortress with determination as she thought about all the ways her plan could go sideways. She needed to get to London fast before the Tribunal found out she had their worst nightmare.

Kieran never knew real quiet until he had to drive back to Renegades by himself. Even though London never spoke to him while they ventured through town, her malice spoke loud enough for the both of them. Now, he sat at a red light long enough to let the self-loathing build in his chest. Kieran never allowed the feeling to reach this level but here it was, knocking at his door. If he were a lesser man, he would let it consume his every waking thought.

Instead, he allowed the light to turn green. He allowed a lot of things to happen lately that should never have taken place. He had allowed himself to care for a woman who had no place in the world and yet she still demanded a seat at the table. Of all the things London Reign wasn't, she was not afraid to let her true emotions shine through. That was what got her in trouble in the first place.

Now it was Kieran's feelings that needed to be reined in. The play on words was not lost on him as she pulled into the mostly empty parking lot. For a Saturday night, it wasn't as packed. That could have something to do with the fact the Garden was running a special that cut five dollars off the admission price to any couple coming in to enjoy a little sin.

Italian leather shoes splashed into a puddle from a rainstorm Kieran hadn't been aware happened. The clouds rolled above him accompanied by thunder and lightning. A storm was definitely brewing both in the heavens and on Terra. It didn't matter which won. The only thing that mattered was finding London and talking some sense into her.

The sound of house music flooded the room with the twist of the knob. The night was fast approaching and the only people that Kieran saw standing at the bar were Jaxon, Mason, and Dom.

"The gang's all here."

His sarcasm was evident to all occupants already present as Mason held up amber liquid without a word. No words needed to be spoken at the moment. Kieran had royally screwed up and he was aware it would take a whole lot of ass-kissing and groveling to make it up.

Candy told him that Simon had befriended her using a different name. Wes. It had become Kieran's mission to figure out why neither himself nor Jaxon realized one of their employees was living a double life. Not to mention why Simon would go to such lengths to win a game Kieran wasn't playing.

"I fucked up."

"I know," was all that Mason said.

"What do you mean? How do you know?"

Mason downed another shot that didn't go down as smooth as he would have liked. The small cough that accompanied it only served to delay his next words, which were, "I ran into London on the way out of your place. I wasn't spying. I just needed some advice about Chastity and she came barreling out talking about you being a man whore."

The groan that left Kieran spoke volumes as the rest of the room chuckled. The rest of the crew was milling around making themselves busy while also listening in at the same time.

"Don't y'all have somewhere to be?" Kieran's voice raised loud enough for everyone to hear him.

Each employee did have a prior engagement because they each took off like a fire being lit under them. Good. Kieran needed to hold some respect, and fear among his employees.

"I met her briefly," Dom chimed in.

"What'd you think?"

"I think whatever you did, you need to un-fuck it."

"What does that even mean, Dom?" Jaxon chuckled trying his best to ignore the daggers being thrown his way.

"It means take whatever it is you fucked up and undo it. Before it's too late."

Kieran heard her loud and clear but how was he supposed to undo anything when he didn't know where she was? His calls instantly went to voicemail, which meant she turned her phone off. He had been able to track her for a while but now that was finished too. She didn't want to be found and he did not respect that.

"I just need—"

"Stone."

Kieran's name was spoken with an authority he hadn't heard in years. The last time he heard his name spoken that way it was to offer him a second chance at life in Cerbi. In the end, it was a hybrid type of life but Kieran would take what he could.

"Diablo?"

"We need to talk."

Lucas St. Claire stood in the middle of the dance floor with his combat boots on looking like a soldier time had forgotten. His fatigues weren't made for comfort or style. They were made for functionality. His skin reminded Kieran of London's sienna tone and for the first time when he looked at his mentor, he saw his daughter too.

"Now's not the time or place."

"Now's the only time," Lucas's voice was stern as he stepped forward to get his point across.

"What about—?" the question cut short with the wave of Lucas's hand.

"We're gonna need all of them if we're gonna get London back."

Kieran's heart dropped at the words that left Lucas's mouth.

If we're gonna get London back.

"What does that mean?"

"It means the worst has happened. The Tribunal knows about my baby girl. London's been taken."

Kieran thought he knew fear. Nothing compared him for the horror he felt as he heard his mentor say the words he never thought possible. He had been careful to hide her, yet she had fallen in their hands anyway. What did he expect? The house always won.

TWENTY-SEVEN

Metal scraped the floor waking London from a restless sleep. Pain coursed through her hand reminding her of earlier events. It felt like hours after Raphael disappeared before she was able to close her eyes. Footsteps echoed softly on the dirty floor coming to a halt directly in front of her.

London contemplated pretending to sleep. She didn't know what would happen if they were aware she was awake. Maybe if she kept her eyes closed whoever it was would leave. With any luck she could catch them off guard and try to escape. The throbbing in her wrist reminded her why her plan was a terrible idea.

"He told us to stay away from her. I've heard the stories about her family and none of them end with, and they lived happily ever after."

"Quit your whining. Bitch can't be that bad if she's in here. I'm sure they just want to keep her here until Wes can get the Broker here. Heard her kind can fetch a pretty penny."

"You think?"

London knew Raphael's voice but who was this new man? Not wanting to risk being found out, London slowly opened one eye until the two men came into view. Raphael stood there with his back to her lecturing a man with the same round build as him. He was a new guard from the way he spoke to Raphael with hesitance and fear.

"Do you believe everything Wes tells you?" Raphael scoffed. "Besides, if she is gone tomorrow who will know?"

This train of thought seemed to slowly make its way through the young man's mind as his gaze slowly moved toward London. Even with the dirt and bruises, he looked at her with lust. The sound of metal rippling down metal resonated in her ears as the door was pushed closed behind them.

The decision had been made. They were going to finish what Raphael had started earlier. Only this time Eric wasn't around to smack some sense into him.

The sound of a zipper being pulled down fell on deaf ears. Dingy blue jeans dropped to the ground kicking up another round of dust. Shortly after underwear followed and London knew this nightmare was slowly becoming her new reality.

Her breath caught in her throat as she said a silent prayer that whatever happened next would happen soon. As awful as it sounded, she just wanted to rip the Band-Aid off.

Closing both eyes again, London said a silent prayer before slowly opening her eyes to the sound of keys jingling.

"What are you doing?"

"Can't have her like this, chained to the wall. Besides, there's two of us and it looks like the bitch is hurt," the new guard laughed mentioning the obvious state of her wrist.

London's eyes popped open to see a large phallic shape in front of her face. Her captor fumbled with the handcuff keys as the mushroom-shaped head cried tear after tear. Each one rolled down the shaft and disappeared into the bush of hair that lay nestled close to his body.

"Donovan, leave it."

So that was his name.

Finally free, London's hand fell with a loud thud causing her to cry out. "Bitch is awake finally."

Without a second thought, Raphael pushed Donovan to the side and stepped up to a whimpering London.

The glint in his eyes told her there was no room to argue.

"You know what to do bitch." He smiled, moving his hips side to side. London looked up into hazel eyes that held no remorse. There was only hatred for all women, herself included now.

When she didn't move to place his member into her mouth, Raphael's large fingers threaded through her black locks. A hard tug moved her head back causing her to scream as a firm hand made contact with her face.

"I said, you know what to do bitch. Now do it," he snarled pulling London forward.

The tip of the mushroom-shaped head touched London's mouth, demanding entrance as she peered up at him. When she once again refused to open her mouth, Raphael hit her again harder than before. Hard enough that she knew it would leave a bruise.

The air around her shifted and grew warmer. She felt pressure pushing down on her chest as she slowly opened her mouth.

"That's it."

The sudden sound of shuffling caught Raphael's attention as he looked away from London for a brief second, "What the fuck are you doing? Wait your turn."

"Raph—I don't know if this is a good idea after all. Something's off man. I can feel it," he stammered as sweat began to bead on his forehead.

"You're just nervous. Wipe the sweat away, watch and learn, okay?" He laughed.

"Nah. I'm gonna take off," Donovan stammered again.

No matter what Raphael thought, London could tell Donovan believed the stories just a little. Especially now that the air around him felt humid. Not to mention the sweat that was profusely rolling down his face. Not all beautiful packages held sugary surprises.

The chubby man ran a hand over his wet brow, removing another set of droplets. He hadn't stopped sweating since Raphael had demanded the girl suck him off. His five-foot-eight-inch frame swayed slightly as he tried to keep from throwing up.

His nerves finally took over where his arrogance once was. His eyes darted back to the woman covered in dirt and ash.

"Fine. Get the fuck out of here. More for me." Raphael laughed watching the equally chubby man turn to hightail it out.

One, two, three tugs later, and the door did not budge. "It won't open man. I thought it locked from the outside, not the inside. It won't fucking open."

Outside the wind howled at the heavens, begging it to end the night, and yet the wind raged on. That hadn't stopped Raphael from walking down two flights of stairs to force himself on London as she sat helpless on the floor. That was the name she heard through the door before he decided to ignore his friend and barge in any way.

Another slap caused London's eyes to sting, but she refused to cry. Instead, she took a deep breath and looked up into the face of the man looming over her. His mouth opened and moved rapidly, but no words were coming from them. Everything around London had slowed down and she felt a familiar pressure. She knew this feeling all too well. Something bad always followed.

A fire building in the pit of her stomach she \ only just found out existed coursed through her veins. In mere seconds, the temperature in the room shot up from humid to an inferno. Small beads of sweat popped up on her forehead and trailed down to her cheeks.

Ignoring his surroundings and the shrill yells of his coworker, Raphael looked down at London and began to laugh.

"Don't worry little girl. If you're good I won't hurt you too badly. Now open your fucking mouth!"

This time when London's eyes met the veined member staring her in the face she moved forward slightly. Green veins snaked under beige skin, pulsing slowly with each pass of blood. Confined to the elongated object that jutted toward here. Silently begging her to swallow it whole.

Flames danced behind copper eyes as they slowly began to glow marigold. It appeared only the amulet around Simon's neck worked. Were there even drawings on the walls and door outside the room?

Oblivious to what was going on below him, Raphael looked at Donovan behind him and let out a boisterous laugh.

"Fucking pansy, just leave already."

"Oh my god," Donovan whispered as he looked past Raphael's half-naked body.

"What now?"

London listened to Raphael let out a scream as hot embers embraced his member. The last thing he saw was flames, as the fire moved over London's hand.

"Who's the bitch now!" she screamed as the concrete beneath her became scorched and the screams within the confines of the room became louder until they finally faded into nothing.

TWENTY-EIGHT

Georgia Rae never thought of herself as a criminal. She thought of herself as a harbinger of excellent virtue, filled with love, light, and truth. Today, she was none of those things. As she watched the trees zoom by in a blur of chartreuse and tangerine, Georgia Rae couldn't ignore the gnawing feeling trapped in her gut. She tried to do the right thing in the end to some degree.

Eve would be arriving somewhere in the vicinity, close enough that once Georgia Rae's task was complete she could take a Conduit straight to her. It would also give Georgia Rae enough time to escape with her riches in hand, away from Wes.

Wes.

She almost forgot about him in the moment. But Georgia Rae knew that was dangerous. Wes killed people, and on any other occasion, he might consider bestowing the same fate on Georgia Rae. Five million dollars was allowing her to remain among the land of the living. Five million reasons to ensure she didn't fall prey to a serial killer with nothing to lose and everything to gain.

Georgia Rae's assistant Amelia was equally as quiet. That wasn't unusual. Georgia Rae liked it more when Amelia didn't speak. It wasn't because she found her voice to be shrill or even obnoxious. Georgia Rae hated for her assistant to speak because the majority of her ideas were brilliant. Had she acknowledged any of Amelia's ideas, Georgia Rae would be out of an assistant. And she couldn't bear to think of someone else organizing her life. Amelia did an amazing job, and Georgia Rae was too selfish to allow her to become great.

Selfish?

Definitely.

The black Lincoln town car came to an abrupt stop. For a moment, Georgia Rae wanted to let loose an array of swears but kept to her demure demeanor. Rusted metal invaded every square inch of the alleyway that hid the vehicle among aluminum siding and broken windows. The name Miller's stamped in a muddled brown that faded with time.

"We're here Mrs. Devereux."

"And where is here?" Georgia Rae tried to keep the disgust from her voice as manicured hands lowered the window a few inches.

"The warehouse district."

Georgia Rae never ventured to this particular portion of town, but she knew it well. The warehouse district was where the city moved the homeless. The mayor had dedicated a portion of her campaign to clean up the city. Her slogan to win back our streets spread like wildfire among the affluent communities until, one by one, each homeless individual was relocated.

Unhoused individuals, Georgia Rae reminded herself.

"Let's get this over with," Georgia Rae huffed pushing up her Prada sunglasses. A little cliché, but what did she care? When one was as rich as the Devereux family, impracticalities meant nothing.

The air was a little warmer tonight. It reminded her of what the weather in New Haven should feel like. Her signature Louboutins clicked against the uneven surface and continued up the grated stairs. Georgia Rae prayed her heels didn't fall between the metal slats that also clanged beneath her feet.

Once inside, stale air and water assaulted Georgia Rae's nostrils. The smell of smoke wrapped around her body like a weighted blanket until it seeped into her clothing.

"Do you have my money?"

Georgia Rae's hand moved to her chest at the echo of a man's voice. Her eyes darted around but found there was no one within view.

"I do." She held out the bag, knowing that it was a lie, before continuing with, "Now you."

The voice could only belong to Wes, her favorite serial killer. When there was no answer, Georgia Rae continued with, "You'll get your money when I get the girl."

"The girl is downstairs behind a reinforced metal door. But I don't think you want to see her right now."

"And why is that?"

Which only garnered the word, "Listen."

For the first time, Georgia Rae allowed the silence around her to become deafening. Only then did she hear what Wes wanted her to.

Screaming.

"What—"

"I don't know what god-forsaken thing you had me kidnap, but I aim to kill it."

"Kill her and you get nothing," Georgia Rae replied sounding a lot braver than she felt.

"Or I could just kill you, too."

"Kill me and you won't get all of your money."

The room was quiet except for the last of the screaming which eventually died out as well. "So that is not my five million."

The sentence was a statement.

"What do you want her for anyway?"

"That's not important."

"I suppose not." Simon smiled moving into the light.

"Wait—I know you," Georgia Rae gasped. It was the young man from Renegades.

"You don't know me, but I know you," Simon taunted.

"What's the meaning of this?"

"Let's go over the meaning, Mrs. Devereux. I think you are scared of me. Because you are scared, I think that you do indeed have my five million dollars."

"I—"

"And because you have my money, the meaning is that unless you give me a good reason—you're both gonna die."

It was at this moment Georgia Rae was thankful she had her backup plan in place. Although she had hoped to be in the wind when Eve arrived, she was thankful when a Conduit opened and three individuals stepped through.

"What in the hell is that?" Georgia Rae heard Simon or Wes ask.

"Thank god, you're here."

The only individuals that Georgia recognized were the Collector Khaiv "Eve" Rexton and Kieran Alexander. The other woman was a mystery to her, but at the moment she was okay with letting some mysteries remain unsolved.

"Where is my daughter?"

"Daughter?" Georgia Rae's voice collided with the mystery woman as she looked from each person. Both questions were voiced back-to-back, and neither was answered.

"Hi, Ms. Reign." Simon smiled, it seemed he was enjoying the new company, "Where's your other half?"

"I can see why Kieran wants to knock you on your ass," Ruby volunteered. "Now where is my daughter?"

Georgia Rae decided at that moment now was as good as any to make her escape.

Who was she to get in the way of a family reunion.

London waited for mortification to fill her. She had just killed a man. When relief washed over her instead, she allowed a small chuckle to escape. She had controlled the fire; it hadn't controlled her. London had taken the lessons Kieran taught her and used it against the fire, and she had come out victorious.

But even small victories come at a cost. And for exerting so much of her ability came when her body collapsed near the charred body. The crackle and pop of flesh should have made her sick, but the adrenaline hadn't worn off yet.

The threat of pain lingered under the surface moving from her wrist to her shoulder. She knew she'd feel that later, but first she needed to free herself.

When the would-be rapist entered the room, he had given her the perfect way out. The door was closed but it wasn't locked anymore.

"Oh my god."

The gasp was followed by the sound of someone vomiting, a woman. "Help me!"

Her prayers had been answered. She watched a woman old enough to be her mother slowly walk down the stairs and stop mere feet from the body. Not body…bodies. The assailant's friend had been caught in the crossfire too, and for a moment London wanted to feel sad but all she could think was good riddance.

"London?"

"Yes. I was kidnapped by a crazy person. Can you get me out of here?"

"Did you do all of this?" the woman asked turning her eyes back toward the charred men.

Dread filled London as she watched the woman dressed in black take a step around each individual until she was only a few feet away.

"My name's Georgia Rae. Your family is here, but before I help you, I need something from you."

"Something like what?"

In London's experience people never asked her for something she was willing to give. Now felt like the same kind of request as her eyes shifted toward the open door.

"I don't have anything to give."

"But you do," Georgia Rae answered pulling a syringe from her purse.

London's fight or flight kicked in but not before Georgia Rae was able to pierce her skin with the needle and pull a decent amount of blood from her body. The chain reaction that the pain caused allowed London's hands to glow white for the first time since she had been captured.

"I'd leave now," London warned not wanting another death on her hands.

"Thank you."

London knew Georgia Rae wasn't thanking her for sparing her life. This small act of gratitude felt like something she would come to regret in the future. The quick tap, tap, tap of her heels echoed in London's ears as the glow mixed with flames. And for the first time since she began to control her abilities, London was able to focus her energy on one spot.

Outside the sound of music wafted toward her through broken glass that was too high to escape from.

No amount of screaming would allow anyone outside to hear her. And from her surroundings, London wasn't sure anyone would come to her rescue anyway.

When nothing happened and the pain began to return, London closed her eyes and began to breathe in her nose and out her mouth. She imagined the fire and her aura mixing together. The marigold and alabaster ribbons formed a tornado around her wrist.

Now that London knew there was no barrier, she closed her eyes and focused before whispering, "Aperta."

The sound of screaming drifted into the room once the door cracked open. London stood on unsteady legs as she cradled her broken arm and moved toward the metal stairs. They either led to freedom or death.

And death wasn't an option.

TWENTY-NINE

Kieran wouldn't be happy until Simon was dead. He orchestrated the destruction of his relationship with London and then kidnapped her. If Simon touched one hair on her head, there'd be nothing left for anyone to identify once Kieran was done.

Yes, he would make Simon pay. And when the time came, he'd kill him and anyone else involved. That included Georgia Rae Devereux.

"What brings you here?" Simon toyed with their emotions and Kieran didn't care much for his bullshit.

"You know why we're here! Where is London?!"

"First of all, take the bass out of your voice!" Simon's voice boomed back at Kieran, "Secondly, London is okay—for now."

"What does that mean?"

"Just what I said. If I get what I want, then London is free to go, but seeing as my financier has given us the slip, it's starting to look a little bleak."

Kieran's eyes moved to the left to see Georgia Rae was no longer there. He needed to find London quick.

"Where is London?" Kieran asked calmer than he felt.

"She's hanging around here somewhere," Simon quipped. Kieran could tell he was deriving satisfaction out of the panic that wafted off everyone but Eve.

"What do you want?" Eve interjected; arms folded across her bosom.

"I want that abomination cleansed from this world."

"Hand her over and I guarantee she will never be anyone else's problem."

Kieran wasn't sure if Eve meant the words that spewed from her mouth. She was a member of the Tribunal and as such it was her duty to bring London in.

"How do I know that?"

Kieran knew Simon was an asshole, but he never thought he was fucking crazy. The body language alone screamed he was ready to blow. Kieran needed to proceed with caution or the situation would become volatile.

"Besides, I was promised a finder's fee and you let that bitch get away with it."

"Money is not a problem. We can get you money."

"Five million dollars worth?" Simon scoffed. He was right, there was no way Kieran could scrap together that much money to give away on such short notice.

"One way or another we will get London and then you can go straight to hell."

"Come get her," Kieran heard right before Simon ran toward him making contact with his fist.

Kieran's vision went blurry as tears filled his eyes. He squeezed his eyes shut tight, a grimace crossing his face. Kieran ignored the pain the best he could, striking out in retaliation. The sound of Simon grunting was music to Kieran's ears. If he caused even an ounce of pain, he called that a victory.

Panic took over for a moment as another blow contacted Kieran's stomach. His body doubled over hitting the ground with a thud.

"Get up!"

The heel of Simon's steel toed boots made contact with Kieran's side, the release of air foreign to his ears. The ringing was still present from the hit he took moments before.

"Fuck—you," the gasp left Kieran's mouth accompanied with a string of blood.

Simon looked down at him with a smirk. Kieran didn't want to think of what demented pleasure he was deriving from his pain.

"Still got your tough guy act, I see?" Simon's face was inches from Kieran's face as he taunted him.

"You have no idea," Kieran whispered reaching up to grab his head sending a pulse through it.

The next blow connected with Simon's face. The yell was sweet music to Kieran's ears.

"I used to feel sorry for you." Kieran's large frame leaned down, a triumphant smile still plastered on Simon's face.

"Why's that?" Simon stayed on his back, a small chuckle escaping him.

"For being such an asshole. And now you're going to die."

"Oh yeah. How?"

"Hopefully, slowly. Now!"

Before he could say anything, another Conduit opened and gunshots rang out. Kieran threw his body to the ground covering his head for protection. What good would that do? A bullet didn't have a name on it. It only held pain and sorrow.

Lucas St. Claire stepped through with a rifle slung over his body as he aimed for Simon.

"Enough!" The scream erupted from all around them as London's voice entered the room.

"You must be London," a voice chimed in.

Realization set in and London whispered, "Diablo?"

London needed to play it smart. She could see the darkness, better known as Eve standing in the room as well. She didn't want to give away the fact that her father was Lucas.

"How do you know this name," Eve questioned.

"Kieran mentioned his mentor. There's a photo of the two of them."

London couldn't believe her eyes. Her father was standing a few feet from her.

"I have so many questions for you." For a moment Kieran thought he saw Lucas take a step in London's direction.

"How about we get out of here first." Kieran watched London's hands move up as she chanted under her breath until Simon began to scream and his hand caught fire.

Dropping to the floor he was able to extinguish the flame quickly before throwing his body behind a stack of crates. Not the safest hiding place, but it would do in a pinch.

Kieran needed to draw attention from London. She still didn't have full control of her abilities and one wrong move could put them all in the hospital and kill Simon before he had his questions answered. Kieran needed to know how Georgia Rae fit into this situation. He needed to know more about Simon or Wes.

"You gonna let your man fight your battles now, Lonny?" Simon taunted, his voice coming from a different portion of the warehouse.

"You know, I always hated that nickname."

"Even better."

"Kieran, you need to go."

"I'm not leaving you," Kieran answered standing in the middle of the room. Wherever Simon was, he would gladly switch places with London in a heartbeat. But Kieran had a feeling he couldn't negotiate with someone so unhinged.

"How about I take you both," he heard Simon counter.

Pain flared once more as every muscle in Kieran's body tensed up. He strained to keep standing, his eyes focused on London. With the nod of his head she released the arm she cradled and lifted her hand in Simon's general direction.

"Incendius."

The incantation still caught Kieran off guard as the room was set ablaze. "Open a Conduit. Go."

"London!"

"Trust me Mom," London yelled at the sound of her mother's voice. Ruby had remained quiet for the duration of the standoff, entering quietly after everyone else, but Kieran had a feeling she was about to unleash her wrath on everyone deemed a threat to her daughter. If it meant her daughter was giving herself up to a psychopath, then Kieran had a feeling Ruby Reign would be out for blood.

"Trust me!" London yelled toward Kieran again.

The Conduit appeared out of nowhere. A large portal that had no beginning or end. "What the —"

"Enjoy the heat, Simon. May you burn in hell. Go!"

Kieran waited until London was in front of him to take off toward the Conduit. The last thing he heard was the sound of Simon's screams.

THIRTY

Fire coursed through London's arm chased by ice water. It was a sensation she never experienced before, pain at war with relief. She wasn't sure which one she wanted to win, but for a brief second, she wished the fire would consume her. She deserved to feel the pain. It was her fault everyone's life were placed in jeopardy. Simon and Georgia Rae wanted her and everyone else was collateral damage.

London squeezed her eyes shut tighter and willed the fire to ignite in her veins and burn through her soul until there was nothing left.

The gentle throbbing in her wrist mingled with the silent rhythm in her head. The pain like a silken scarf wrapped in bongo drums and then coated with shards of glass reminded her she went through a horrible ordeal. Each thump was bittersweet filled with the drone of beeping in the background. No, the pain was worth it if it reminded her not to be a victim.

It was annoying but it was also a small price to pay for being alive. London's fingers twitched involuntarily as another chill ran through her arm. Though it tried, the ice water did nothing to quench the fire's thirst. Instead, it raged on, battling the freezing temperature of the water, creating jagged bolts of pain.

London tried to move her fingers on her own, but the pain stopped that experiment from taking place. The haze clouding her mind began to lift and with it, the fire in her wrist grew, a sluggish grunt the only sound to signal she was finally awake.

"London!"

All her efforts to open her eyes failed as she heard a woman shushing her, the cold chill of liquid numbing her fingers again as the ice water mixed with fire once more.

"Breathe, Sam."

"Stone?"

"The nice doctors need you not to burn down this building."

Tears fell from London's eyes as she listened to the sound of his voice. "I'm glad you found me," she whispered as her eyes drifted shut. She could finally dream in peace and replace a sliver of happiness with the pain and darkness that dwelled behind her eyelids.

Simon kidnapped her and Georgia Rae had gotten away.

"I need to help find the woman who took my blood."

"You need to stay put," Kieran whispered a look of confusion on his face.

"It's all my fault though. I didn't know. It's all my fault."

"What about Simon?"

"Got away."

"That's impossible. I heard his screams."

"The warehouse burned to the ground, that's for sure. But when the fire department got there they only found the remains of charred remains of what they believe are two men in a subbasement. Neither was Simon.

"So, he got away?"

"It looks like it."

"But how?"

London stared blankly at him before asking, "And the lady in black?"

"Georgia Rae?"

"Is that her name? She took my blood and left me there to die."

"She's in the wind, too."

"Let's hope she stays that way." London's eyes moved back toward her bandaged wrist. She had her life and Kieran; life should be good. Instead, she was in a hospital bed secretly hating herself.

"Sam, are you okay? Do you need the nurse?"

"No, just you."

The smirk that crossed his face looked bittersweet, but that was how their story started.

Whether she was supposed to have a happy ending was irrelevant, London Reign knew the fire that threatened to kill her was only the beginning.

Visiting hours ended at ten. The fight to get everyone to leave was a long and arduous one, but London convinced the nurse to kick everyone out, including her mother. The glow from the television played shadows across her face. The volume didn't need to be on, London wasn't paying attention to it anyway.

"I don't know how you summoned me here, but I'm impressed."

London's eyes moved to the corner to find Eve there shrouded by darkness.

"I didn't, Kieran did," she confessed. "I asked him to leave once it was done. This conversation is only for the two of us."

"What can I do for you, your Highness," sarcasm dripped from Eve's voice.

"God, that sounds awful. Just London, please."

The chuckle that followed was laced with malice. "You have some nerve calling me here. You aren't supposed to be here."

"So I've been told. But I want to make it right."

"The only thing that could make this right is you standing trial within the Citadel."

"We both know how that ends for me and my mother. And I refuse to let you sentence us to death."

"Not just your mother. Funny how we still don't know your father's identity."

"Hear me out and it won't matter what my father's name is. Like I said, I want to make it right. A way that even the Tribunal will approve of."

Silence always followed London when she made bold statements like the one that just left her mouth.

"What do you mean? There is only a cell on Styxx. What could you offer us?"

"For the last five years, my mother has taught me about her family. It wasn't until this year I learned more about my father."

"And who exactly is your father," Eve coaxed.

London simply smiled and continued, "As the daughter of both a Highborne and a Collector my bloodline is intertwined with royalty and a need to be of service. What if I renounce one? Is that possible?"

"No."

"If I contracted a Beldame to perform another Shift it could be."

"Are you not already indebted to one Beldame?"

"No," London answered without any explanation.

Eve's eyes moved to London's face to find no deception present. There was only determination.

"And what will this Beldame do for you?" Eve asked before following her question up with, "Be careful, a request like this comes with a steep price."

"I know the price one must usually pay, but I have a counteroffer that I don't think anyone would turn down."

"I'll be the judge of that."

"I want to have died."

"What games are you playing, London Reign?"

"No games. I want the Shift to go back to the day I died and erase my Resurrection. As far as anyone would be concerned, London Reign died on her twenty-fifth birthday. That's what the Tribunal wants, correct? Me . . . dead."

Silence.

"I know nothing can turn back time. What is fated shall be. But I have read up on a lot since my mother began training me, and the Shift makes the most sense in this situation."

"The Tribunal would still remember."

"But everyone beyond in Chaos would forget, correct?"

Eve thought for a moment before she said, "It's a possibility."

"Great."

"And you are willing to pay the price for this? The possibility that one day a Beldame will call upon you to forfeit the life of a member of your family in exchange for her life?"

"Yes. My only stipulation if you accept is once it is all done, you recruit me."

Laughter bubbled up from Eve's chest as she looked down at the injured Eldite. "Recruit you?"

"As much as you hate me, my bloodline is still half Collector, and it is my birthright. I hereby formally denounce my right to any throne as a Highborne. I give my life to Adon. May his will be with me."

Again, Eve looked into London's eyes, taking in the serious expression behind her copper expression.

"Why now?" Eve asked

"Why not?" London countered.

"Okay, London, we can do it your way. Just know, there is no going back."

"I know, and from now on call me Sam."

"Sam," Eve smiled, "I like it."

EPILOGUE

London felt like the villain in a rewritten fairytale told to warn children around the world. Only she wasn't the beautiful princess fighting for her life, she was the evil queen. The Tribunal was satisfied for the moment, but there was no way they'd let a fully functioning Eldite exist. Whether she wanted to acknowledge it or not, London was living on borrowed time.

Life on Cerbi wasn't without its ups and downs, the council members just beyond Cerbi borders all sharpened their pitchforks waiting for the day she decided to kill them all. The only thing any of them had to go on was legend and rumors of a time no one was around to witness.

There was no longer talk of war and violence because the fear was removed with a simple spell. Well, not simple, but effective. Memories of a young girl plagued with a burden too great to handle were erased within moments and replaced by memories of a happier time. A new aura was given to follow the Vlosyrós Laws.

"Praise Adon."

The chant could be heard throughout the province as London Reign officially died and Sam was born. Eve stood before the Tribunal with a half-smile as she nodded her head in recognition, London had officially renounced her Highborne status and abilities. The turn of events should have saddened London, but in the end, the fresh start was exactly what everyone needed. Her family would be better off without her.

The Shift ensured everyone in Terra had forgotten London ever existed that included her mother, Ruby. To the world, London Reign died on her twenty-fifth birthday. Eve carried out her part of the deal with the only stipulation being Kieran could not be the one who Collected her. Other than that, the world continued to spin as if nothing was amiss. London pulled off the impossible.

London's only regret was knowing that her mother had mourned her. Ruby thought she would be resurrected, but thanks to the Shift, Ruby dug up a grave only to find her daughter was still dead.

It wasn't fair, but life wasn't fair and all things were up to Adon. And one way or another, Adon always won.

"Sam, how are you adjusting?"

"As well as I can, I suppose," London answered while checking in on her family from the Veil.

"Glutton?"

"Hmm?"

Eve's only response was a nod toward the mirror before the images within disappeared. "Hey!"

"Sam, to leave London behind, you have to let her die. You have to die."

"I did die."

"But no one knows you exist in this form. London Reign, a Human woman died. You had no friends. You had no love to mourn you and you have no family waiting on you. That was the choice you made for them, and it is a choice you need to accept or this Shift will all be for nothing."

London knew what Eve said was true. To embrace her new life as Sam, she would have to let the shell of herself truly fade into nothing. She had watched her mother mourn her and now it was time to do the same thing.

"Are you ready to let go of London?"

Never.

"Yes."

"London?" a familiar voice echoed behind the two women. All the air left London's lungs as she waited for the sound of footsteps to depart. When they didn't recede she turned her face to see Jaxon standing there.

"Hi. I'm Sam," London smiled extending her hand.

What the hell happened?

"Eve just called you London," Jaxon frowned staring at the outstretched hand.

Confusion marred Jaxon's face as he finally took the outstretched hand, a mistake London hadn't counted on as her thoughts screamed into his head.

"What was that?!"

"Shit! No one can know Jax. I'm not even sure you know what you saw."

"How?"

"Jaxon—"

"Don't fucking lie to me!"

"It's a long story, but you can't let anyone know you remember."

"The fuck I can't! Do you know how I got here London?"

"Jax—"

Someone destroyed Renegades trying to look for you. I wasn't supposed to be there, but that didn't stop them from beating the shit out of me."

"What? No—"

"Thankfully, no one else was seriously hurt but my injuries were pretty bad. That was what some woman explained. She gave me two options. Succumb to my injuries and move into some place called the Veil or join her and become a Collector. I chose option two."

"Oh god."

"Adon, right? She said most people choose option two when given the choice."

"I know you're angry right now Jaxon, but—" London began.

"You don't know shit."

It wasn't fair, but there was nothing she could do about it. Jaxon didn't care about fairness and laws at this moment, she knew that. He hated her and London would need to learn how to be okay with gaining a new enemy.

"Jaxon...I won't say I'm sorry because you wouldn't believe me, so hate me if you must. I can take it."

The gravel from her voice resonated in the room, bouncing off every surface until it landed on Jaxon, his body tense from her words. His eyes were the same shade as Kieran's, only these eyes looked through her, these eyes hated her.

"How kind of you," Jaxon whispered, his gaze moving from her face.

"Duerme," London whispered catching Jaxon as his body went limp. She hadn't put someone to sleep before, it was kind of cool.

"What was that?" Eve demanded.

"Nothing. He was asking questions about London."

"You can still do Chaos Magic?"

"Just a little. It's no big deal"

"No, it's a game changer." Eve swore under her breath.

"Jaxon's here?"

"Fuck me," London whispered under her breath as Kieran walked up behind her.

"I'm afraid we have a bigger problem. London's ability isn't bound. Once the rest of the Tribunal finds out it won't be Styxx for her. It'll be death."

"What should I do?"

London stared at Eve with a shocked expression.

"Run and don't stop running. I'll give you a head start, but once the other council members find out we won't rest until you're dead. That includes your mother."

It looked like time was running out for London after all.

Fuck.

ABOUT THE AUTHOR

Bridgett Evans is a native of Arkansas but currently resides with her family in Texas. *Fire and Reign* is her debut novel. When she's not writing, Bridgett enjoys spending time with her husband and their two children.

ACKNOWLEDGMENTS

I would like to thank Elizabeth Cartwright for posting the magnificent that would become the cover for Fire and Reign. Her cover embodied everything I wanted my story to convey with just a glance.

To my editor, Megan Joseph, thank you for believing in my book with such conviction that you pushed me to think outside the box. Without her questions and insight, the plot would have fallen flat.

And to save the best for last, I'd like to thank my husband Manny Santoyo. His motivation got me through every stage of the writing process. He gave me words of encouragement when I had none. He ensured I had a quiet space to think and was the best Muse.

Printed in the USA
CPSIA information can be obtained
at www.ICGtesting.com
CBHW020308190424
7163CB00003B/11

9 798218 106805